Secrets of Fortuny Bay

BOOK TWO OF FORTUNY BAY SERIES

ARA GRIGORIAN

© 2023 Ara Grigorian

Printed in the United States of America

First Edition, 2023 - Love Laugh Learn Media

Paperback ISBN-13: 978-1-7324621-7-5
Hardcover ISBN-13: 978-1-7324621-8-2

Covert Art by Virtually Possible Designs

www.AraGrigorian.com

My Family, for putting up with me.

God, for never giving up on me.

Secrets ~ of FORTUNY BAY

Chapter One

Catalina

Cat swiped at her cheeks, wiping the tears. Once again, they'd found a way to take her son away.

Would there come a time when she and Chicho could live out their lives in peace and joy? Would the Roca family ever give up in their yearslong attempt at destroying everything she cared for?

Leo sat next to her on the truck's tailgate and took her hand in his. She glanced at their intertwined hands, then looked up into his eyes.

"I don't believe in no-win scenarios." He turned his attention to where the plumes of dust were still settling around the squad car's tire tracks.

The deputy and the social workers were gone, and so was her child.

"It's just a matter of deciding what we're willing to do to get the victory," Leo said.

Cat blinked. "What are you saying?"

"I am here with you. You are not alone. You are not outnumbered. They were the ones who decided to play dirty. They established the rules. We'll play by their rules."

Cat digested Leo's words.

I am here with you.

You are not alone.

Did he really mean it? Would he really stand with her through it all—no matter what he heard? No matter how ugly things got?

A cool ocean breeze gently fluttered her clothes and hair.

She stared at his hand and felt his confidence. She wanted to believe him. With him, there was a familiarity, a confidence that they had developed when they were younger.

But he'd left her. He'd abandoned her.

Why then would she believe his words now? Had he shown her that he was a changed man now?

Yes, she supposed he had. She couldn't deny that something was happening between them, but that's not what she needed. No, she needed her son back.

Getting Francisco back would not be easy. The court had given her temporary custody until "open matters" from the past were resolved. She was supposed to show them that he belonged with her, that he'd be safe with her, but now they had some trumped-up evidence against her.

She'd do whatever she needed to do. Fight, beg, and everything in between. She'd have to think clearly and plan her next steps. She needed to remain focused on the goal.

She stared into Leo's eyes, then gently pulled her hand out of his.

He blinked, and an unspoken question rose in his gaze.

It hurt her to let go. Maybe because she really did want him next to her through it all. Or maybe because she had lowered her defenses at the worst possible time.

"Talk to me," he said. "What's going through your mind right now?"

She cleared her throat. "We can't win if we play by their rules," she said. "And I don't want to do anything that will prejudice the court."

"What do you have in mind?" asked Lola. Her childhood friend seemed rattled. She'd heard Cat's stories about that family. But hearing and experiencing are very different things.

"Not sure," Cat said to Lola.

He clenched his jaw and ran his hand through his hair. "We can't play nice," he said. "You have to be ready for them to go low. Very low."

She took a deep breath, willing herself to speak, but she didn't have the strength to even start. She placed her hands on the truck's bed to stabilize herself.

"Let's start with our defense. Who's your lawyer?" Leo asked.

She blinked. "I don't have one. I couldn't afford—"

"Well, now you can," he interrupted, then hopped off the truck and turned to Anna. "Who can we get?"

Anna, Leo's right hand at his company who had, without hesitation, come down to Fortuny Bay to help, considered his question.

"Zapata?" he asked.

She shook her head. "He doesn't do family law."

"What about the Greek guy?" he asked.

"No... I think they arrested him for something or other."

Leo flinched. "Crap. Sucks to be him."

"And sucks to be his clients," Anna added.

"What about—" he began.

"Stop," Cat interrupted. "Both of you, please stop."

They faced her.

"I just need some time to think and plan. In silence."

Was a lawyer the solution she needed? Was that really the answer? Or was it time for her to do what she had avoided for years?

She looked to her side. Splayed on the tailgate were the drawings and ideas for how to rebuild the house. Minutes ago, that had been her primary focus. Now, it was a distant and irrelevant idea.

She studied each of their faces. Then forced herself to smile. "Look, I just need to be..."

"Alone?" Leo asked.

Cat glanced at him. The gentleness in his eyes buckled the shield that was trying to form over her heart. He knew that she processed internally. He was the let's-talk-it-out guy. She was not.

"Yeah," she said. "Alone. For a bit."

Silence.

"What can we do?" Anna asked.

She took a deep, strained breath in and, as she exhaled, said what had always been natural.

"Pray," she said, but something deep within her had cracked.

Why had God allowed this to happen to her? Why was an innocent, loving little boy experiencing this type of trauma? She still trusted God. That would not change, but she didn't understand.

And she wondered if she'd be able to overcome this latest attack from her former in-laws. The Roca family would not lose twice. Many had tried. None had succeeded.

Chapter Two

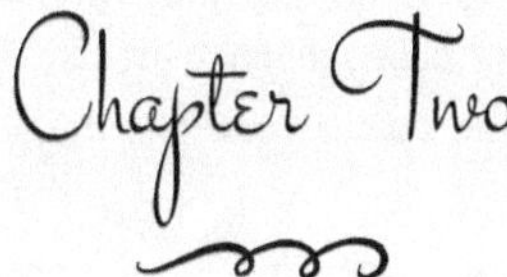

Leo

Leo tapped his fingers on the RV's kitchen table. Lola had left them minutes earlier, and about an hour before that, Cat had locked herself away in the camper's bedroom. She must've been sleeping, resting, or something like that. Was she planning her next move in the quiet of the room? Maybe.

Anna and Leo sat in silence, waiting for... Waiting for what, exactly?

He wanted to be supportive and patient, but what he really felt was annoyed. Cat needed to get up and get things rolling, and she needed a high-power attorney.

The Rocas were not playing around. They had declared war, and he didn't just want to beat them. He wanted to bring that family and this town to their knees for what they were putting Chicho and Cat through.

Leo didn't have a list of enemies, but now, he understood the wisdom of having one. A list with names and the wrongs they've done, and Billy, the deputy...

He placed his hand on his gun. There was no room for forgiveness.

War it is.

As he—impatiently—waited, names of lawyers scrolled through his mind. Those he personally knew and those he'd seen turn the impossible into the possible.

He wanted to call down his helicopter, pick them up, and take them to San Francisco to interview dozens of ridiculously priced lawyers until they found the right attorney.

"We should make a short list," he said to Anna.

She looked up from her phone. "A short list of what?"

He wished more people could read his mind and fill in the blanks for themselves. "Lawyers."

Her brow arched. "Didn't you hear her? She's not ready for that."

"She said she needed time," he said. "Once she's ready, she'll still need a lawyer, and we'll be ready with a short list. She clearly can't defend herself again."

Anna nodded. "Look, I'm with you. I'm trying my best not to jump out of my skin. I'm tempted to get some hired guns—ex-military—and get that poor kid out of wherever he's being held and fly him out of the country."

With each word she spoke, his grin widened. "Okay. Now you're talking my language. That's definitely an option, but we may want to see how things go with the hearing first."

She blinked. "Leo, I was kidding."

He hesitated. "Yeah... me too. Clearly."

"Clearly." She looked over her shoulder. "I've been thinking about some of the logistics. She'll need a place to call home."

He studied her. "Any ideas?"

"First, extend this camper's rental so I can hang out here for the time being. Next, I want to help her with the insurance process. This way, I can be here for her. Particularly since Lola leaves next week. Cat will need someone here."

Leo's chest tightened. He could be here for her, as well, but he suspected that was not what she'd want. When she'd pulled her hand out of his, he understood. She was not going there with him. He wouldn't dwell on that. Not now.

"Let's buy her one of those that have multiple rooms. They're not RVs exactly. They attach to a truck."

"Yup, travel trailers. I know exactly what you're talking about."

"A nice one with at least two bedrooms, a decent-sized kitchen, the whole nine yards. We'd want it delivered and hooked up to the water, electricity, etc. We'll tell her that the insurance approved it."

Anna blinked. "You want to lie to her?"

He shrugged. "It's not really a lie."

She crossed her arms. "I can't wait to see the mental gymnastics you're about to go through to pull off this explanation."

He fidgeted. "Okay, it's an itty-bitty lie. Think of me as her insurance policy against the evils of the world."

"Wow, you really are very impressive at manipulating words."

"Look, she's stubborn. And she has too much on her mind. I'd rather she believes that it's from the insurance so that I don't have to get into another debate as to why she should, and she'll say she can't, and I'll say of course you can, and she'll say—"

"Okay, okay. I got it."

He leaned back, happy with himself. "Now we just have to get her to see the light on that other thing."

At that instant, the bedroom door opened, and out stumbled Cat. Hair disheveled and shirt all wrinkled, Cat joined them at the table. She ran a hand through her hair, then looked at each one for a few seconds. Her eyes were red and her cheeks flushed.

"What *light* is it I need to see?" she asked.

Leo paused, then shifted in his seat.

"Well?" she asked, looking directly into his eyes.

He cleared his throat. "You need a lawyer. And not just any lawyer. You need the type who has gone up against the best of the worst."

She sighed. "You're probably right."

He smiled. "Let's interview a few. Today is almost over. Say, tomorrow?"

She shook her head. "My gut tells me you're right. I need a good lawyer. But I want to find a different angle."

Anna leaned forward. "A good lawyer will find those angles."

Cat sat back, considering. "Look, my suspicion is that the Rocas have never lost in court."

"Say what?" Leo asked.

She shrugged. "I hope I'm wrong. But I don't think I am." She took a deep breath. "When I got Chicho back, that was a setback for them. The look on their faces was almost like gravity had failed to do what it's always done. This time, they'll be ready. And I just have an uneasy feeling that they would not want to go to court unless they were sure of the outcome."

Leo considered the consequences of that—if true. "Do they have influence over the court?"

She shrugged again. "Don't know. But I do think they have more influence than any of us actually realize. But I've been known to be a bit of a conspiracy theorist, so…"

They were all silent for a few moments.

"So, now what?" Anna asked.

"Give me space to think for a couple of days. Child Protective Services will contact me soon. A hearing will be scheduled. Meanwhile, I'll be praying for an answer and a new strategy. I fear that if I come with guns blazing, they will come with tanks. I'd rather they assume I'm not escalating."

Silence. Her approach seemed reasonable. But he wondered if reason is what would win this one. Or would this one require a new, unexpected approach?

"So what can I do?" Leo asked.

She dropped her gaze to her hands, took a deep breath, then looked up at him. "Right now? Nothing. Not until I know more from the court."

"And the house?" he asked.

She shook her head. "I can't focus on that right now. I need to get my son back. The house can and will wait."

He slumped in his seat. That was that, he guessed. In not so many words, she was telling him to butt out for now. So now what was he supposed to do?

Anna cleared her throat. "I plan to stay a bit longer to help button up insurance-related matters. While you focus on Chicho, I'll get them to speed up a temporary living space here on your property. In the meantime, you can bunk up with me in the RV."

Cat offered her a tired smile. "Yeah, that would be amazing."

That made him the odd man out.

"Well…" he started, "then I'll go back for a few days, get some work matters settled while we wait for the next steps."

He studied Cat's eyes, hoping she'd object. Hoping she'd ask him to sleep on that horrible sofa bed in the RV.

"That's a good idea," Cat said instead.

He forced a smile. "I am the ideas guy."

A nearly imperceptible smile appeared on her face.

He'd hold on to that. He'd take whatever she gave him.

Chapter Three

Anna

Anna left the camper and strolled over to the beach. With the sun's gradual descent came the chilly air. The ocean breeze practically cut through her. Her fingers instantly dried up, and the skin of her nose tightened. She knew without a doubt that her nose had turned red.

Anna was a warm weather person. She and the cold were not on speaking terms. Indoors would've been a better option, but she needed to take a walk to sort out her thoughts. She wrapped her arms around herself and found a slice of sand that still had a patch of sun spotlighting it.

She lowered herself to the sand, pulled her knees to her chest, and wrapped herself tightly. She exhaled a sigh of relief.

That's more like it.

Her instincts were on high alert. She was reminded of Shakespeare's *Hamlet*. Something stank around here. Really badly. And no, it was not the marina.

It was in middle school that she became interested in William Shakespeare. When Ms. Schuster read the line from *Henry VI*, "The first thing we do, let's kill all the lawyers," her classmates all agreed that this was because lawyers were bad.

But Anna got what the others hadn't. Dick the Butcher wanted the law out of the way so he could become king. He understood that the law helped the innocent and stopped the corrupt. This is why Anna got into law.

Sitting on the sand in Fortuny Bay, reliving what she had just seen transpire with Chicho and Cat, she could not only smell the corruption, but it also had substance. If Cat was right about the court being bent, then they had a bigger issue than just a custody fight.

The balance was already tipped. This type of corruption was commonplace in authoritarian countries, not small harbor towns in California.

And yet... And yet. The feeling she had was unmistakable. There was more, a lot more to this place. Things were about to get interesting.

And not in a good way.

"What are you doing here?" Leo asked.

She rose to face him. "Planning."

They both studied the breaking waves. One on top of the other, then another and another. Countless layers stacked on top of each other, continually commingling forever.

Leo's phone chimed. He pulled it out, read it, then slid it back into his pocket.

"All good?" she asked.

He nodded. "Yeah. My buddy, the private investigator. I need to tell him to stop digging into my dad's medical history."

She glanced at him. A new idea dawned on her. "Can I work with your PI instead?"

He turned to face her. "What are you up to?"

She grinned. "A hunch."

"Anything you can expand on?"

She shook her head. "Not yet. Because it's just a hunch."

He pulled out his phone, typed something, then hit send. "I told him he reports to you now. I copied you on the email I just sent him. A bit rough around the edges, but he is an expert and gets the work done."

Anna pulled her phone, confirmed that she also had received the message.

"We'll get Chicho back," she said.

He nodded.

She studied his eyes. Were they red? Was he tearing up? This family had really dug themselves into his heart.

"Okay, I'm outta here," he said as he spun away. "I need to hit the road."

"You could stay, you know," she said as they marched back.

"No, I need to be away for a bit. Something's nagging at me, and I'm not sure what it is. I need to create distance to find the perspective I'm missing."

She matched his stride. "Anything specific?"

"Nothing. Everything."

She knew exactly what he meant.

While Leo loaded his belongings into the truck, Anna didn't waste time. She called the investigator.

On the third ring, he responded.

"Yes," he said.

Yes? Is that how you answer the phone?

"Is this Van?" she asked.

A hesitation. "Speaking. Who's this?"

Mister Charming.

"My name is Anna Woods. I work for Leo Moncrieff."

Another brief hesitation. "That's right. He emailed me about you. So...what's up?"

"Van, are you still in the Fortuny area?" she asked.

Silence. "Name's pronounced Van, like Vaughn. Not Van like a minivan."

Anna closed her eyes. *Maybe this was a mistake.*

"Got it," she said. "So...are you in the area?"

"Not exactly. About thirty miles out. I can head your way if you want."

She wasn't sure if things were going to work out with this guy, but Leo would not just hire anyone. "That'll be great. I'll shoot over the address."

After she hung up, she approached Leo as he rolled up the back of the Cybertruck.

"Done?"

He nodded. "Yup."

Something inside the truck caught his attention. He opened the door and pulled loose sheets scattered on the floor and under his seat.

"What's that?" she asked.

"On the night of the fire, someone left these on my windshield." Leo handed her the scanned and printed articles.

She flipped through them quickly to read the headlines.

"They were inside this," he added.

She took the yellow folder from him and inserted the copies inside. "I'll look into these." After she closed the flap, she eyed him. "Any idea who would've left these for you?"

He shrugged. "At the time, I wasn't sure, but given what we know now, it has to be someone from Adela Roca's camp."

"Yes... But who? People like her never do the deed themselves."

He held her gaze. "It could've been a kid. It could've been a delivery service. Why does that matter?"

"Not sure yet. But I suspect that in small towns, all the details matter."

The door to the RV opened. Cat stepped down and headed toward the house.

"Cat," Leo called.

She turned to him.

"I'm taking off," he said.

She blinked. "Right now?"

"Yeah," he said.

She walked up to him and gave him a hug. They seemed so comfortable the way they held each other. Neither looked like they wanted to separate. But she eventually did.

"Thank you for everything," she said.

We joined him as he climbed into his truck, then he faced Cat.

"We'll get him back," he said.

"Absolutely," Anna said.

Cat took a deep breath. "We have to."

A short while later, a brownish gold-colored Toyota Camry from around when she was born pulled up into the driveway. The driver leaned over to the passenger side and manually rolled the window down.

What have I gotten myself into?

"You Anna?" he asked.

His close-cropped hair declared ex-military. His facial hair was either a perfectly groomed beard, or he had one of those faces that produced just the right amount of facial hair. His aviator sunglasses were ridiculous, in her humble opinion.

Okay, fine, they looked good on him, but who other than actors still wore those nowadays?

"In the flesh," she said. "Let's chat somewhere else."

"Hop in," he said.

She took a measured breath, then glanced inside the car. Folders and loose sheets were on the passenger seat. On the floor were cans of energy drinks and empty water bottles. She pointed at them, not knowing exactly what to say.

He looked down. "Ah, crap. Yeah. Hold on," he said as he grabbed a handful of things and tossed them in the back.

She hoped those weren't important. Once he was done, he slapped the seat cushion, presumably to get the dust off.

"Good as new," he said and grinned.

At least he had a pleasant smile. She pulled the handle, but the door didn't respond.

"Gotta yank a bit harder," he said.

She yanked a bit harder, but still nothing.

"Wait up." He stepped out of the car and strolled around the front toward her.

He wasn't tall. Her height, she'd guess. But he had wide shoulders.

She stepped back when he reached the door. When he grabbed the handle, she noticed the tattoo on the inside of his bicep. A mono-colored, ornate cross. Each of the four points of the cross had leafy or floral elements embedded in it.

He flexed, pulled, and the door clanked open. "Needs some WD-40," he said as he held the door open for her.

"It sure needs something," she whispered as she sat on the lumpy chair and pulled the door closed.

He walked around the front of the car, then hopped in. His aftershave wafted in. It was simple. Nice.

She pulled on the seat belt, which was stained with things she didn't want to ask about.

"Let's go to the café to chat," she said.

"That won't work." He dropped the car into first and drove off.

Was that a stick shift? Maybe the car was even older than she had originally estimated.

He pushed it into second, and her head gently whiplashed.

He eyed her. "Not used to manual transmission?"

She shook her head and gave a half smile. "Oh, I've been in other cars that have manual transmission."

"Leo's Spider?" he asked. "That's a sweet ride."

She glanced at him. He'd been in the Spider? Clearly, he was closer to Leo than she had assumed. "Yes, that one...among others. But I can't say I've experienced this class of finely tuned piece of machinery."

He took a quick left, dropped it into a lower gear, then sped up. "She is a beauty," he said, with no sign of humor.

Did he really think she was complimenting the car? If he was so out of touch with reality, she wasn't sure he'd be the right investigator for this job.

She glanced around and realized that she didn't know where they were going. Just as she was about to ask, he pulled into a public park.

"Why here?" she asked. "Why not the café?"

He parked the car, turned off the engine, and jumped out without saying a word.

Mister Personality.

She pulled the handle, but the door did not open. He was about to reach her side. She pulled one more time, then shouldered against it. The door slammed into Van, causing him to hop backward.

"Something I said?" he asked.

Although he didn't smile, she laughed.

She stepped out. "Sorry about that."

"Yeah. No worries." He pointed to a cement table with green fiberglass benches. "Let's go there."

She followed him. The grass was well-maintained, and the overall park was in good shape. Really good shaped. Why would they spend this much money on a park that had barely any use?

In fact, the town was overall very well kept. How did they produce the funds they needed to pay for the upkeep?

When he sat, she took the seat across from him.

She tried again. "Why here?"

He pulled out a cigarette and popped one in his lips. Her face must've betrayed her because he immediately put up a hand.

"Don't worry," he said. "I don't smoke. Not anymore. It's just a thing I do."

She nodded.

He glanced around. "I've been studying this town here for the past few days." The unlit cigarette bounced up and down as he spoke. "Something doesn't feel right."

She leaned in. She had the same feeling but had not been able to put her finger on it. "What do you mean?"

"At first, I thought they're looking at me all weird because I'm a new face. But that didn't work for me. This isn't some two-hundred person town. There are, what, five or six thousand people here. You can't realistically know everyone. And you can't build true groupthink the way you would with very tiny towns. Also, it's a flipping harbor town. You will get unfamiliar faces during the fishing season. The seasonal workers. So why stare at me?"

"Maybe it's those glasses," she threw out.

He stared at her. And even though she could not see his eyes because of those oversized glasses, she knew he was boring into her eyes.

"Hmm," he said, then pulled off the shades. "Better?"

Yes, it was. This man had the brightest blue eyes she'd ever seen. So bright that they hovered into silver. Why would he hide those?

He placed the shades on the table and slid the cigarette back into the box.

"Anyway, I've made a career of blending in," he said. "I work in the shadows and usually, I go unnoticed. But here... Everywhere I went, they saw me." He ran a hand over his head. "Like they knew me...or at least about me. Which is why meeting in the coffee joint was not a good idea. Here, on the other hand," he said, "this place is dead. As beautiful as it is, this park is barely used. Since we're at the planning stage, this place will give us the privacy we need."

She nodded. He was starting to grow on her. "Any theories why this place has caught on to you?"

He shrugged. "They know I'm not one of them. I'm an outsider. And it's clear they don't trust outsiders."

"Why do you think?"

He leaned in. His eyes lit up like beacons. "Only one reason to keep outsiders at a distance. When you've got secrets."

Chapter Four

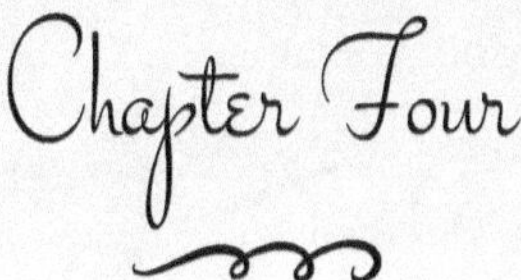

Catalina

Shortly after Leo left, Cat entered the house. This had been their solution—their salvation. Now, it was damaged and uninhabitable.

She carefully walked up the scorched stairs up to Chicho's room. His room had suffered some minor damage.

Cat dragged the closet door open and pulled out all his clothes. She'd have to wash them all to get the smell out. She'd make them perfect again so that when he returned, his favorites would be ready for him.

A fist bore into her stomach. Yes, he would return home. With her. She would not stop until they were together again.

She squeezed the bridge of her nose. No, she would not cry.

Keep going, Cat.

She steadied her breathing. She supposed she could buy him new clothes. She had money now. But these were his. His!

She slumped down on the bed, bunched the clothes in her fists, and brought them to her face. She breathed it all in. Even with the smell of smoke embedded in them, she could smell him. It was faint, but she was sure that scent was his.

She breathed them in again. But this time, he was gone. She turned the shirt over and smelled another spot, then another, and another.

The tears rolled uncontrollably. He was gone. They had him.

And they had her.

She knew they didn't love Chicho. But he was the tool, the device that they'd use against her. A torture device that would put the inventors of pain from the Spanish Inquisition to shame.

Back in the RV, Cat scanned the loot. Clothes, toys, books, and his drawings. She'd done well.

Originally, after the fire, she had decided none of it was worth salvaging. But now, with Chicho gone, she needed anything and everything of his in her possession.

By faith, she believed he'd be back with her. What she didn't know was when and under what circumstances. She never had a problem believing in God's promises, no matter how large or unbelievable. Instead, she struggled with His timing.

She was realistic enough to know that this would end in court. That family would not wake up one morning and decide to return him. What she was praying for was a new strategy, an alternative approach. If not that, then she'd pray for courage and peace.

A court battle would not end well for her. She knew this. Sure, she had some money to fight it out in court. But what she had would disappear in a blink against the money they had.

Leo can outspend them.

No, she would not ask him to do that.

She pulled a batch of his drawings, then sat on the bench. She found Chicho's drawing from the first day Leo arrived. Leo and his truck. A refrigerator in the bed. She and Chicho holding hands.

It had been so much simpler back then. She was not a threat to the Rocas. They had not stepped up the fight because they didn't have to. They were content in keeping her on the faint line between poverty and just making it.

Leo's dad's will had derailed their plan. They had not expected that twist. Nor had she, for that matter.

As much as getting the home and having Leo back in her life had seemed like a blessing, Cat was convinced that this had been the tipping point for the family. They saw a legitimate threat to their objective—humiliate Cat for the rest of her life.

As much as she wanted Leo here with her, she knew that the more he helped, the more damage they would cause. She had to do this on her own. In their domain.

Just the thought of what she was considering gave her chills. But she knew that she'd have to enter the lion's den with humility and extend an olive branch. She'd have to kiss the ring and ask for a pathway.

She was glad Leo was away for now. He would never let her do this, because he didn't really understand what the Rocas were. But Cat did. She had been there for years. She knew.

Cat scrolled through the contacts on her phone and found the name she was looking for. Although the call would get routed to the personal assistant, she understood that by taking this step, she was prepared to agree to do anything to get her child back.

She tapped Adela Roca's name and closed her eyes.

Chapter Five

Leo

For Leo, this was unfamiliar territory. He felt inept. Useless.

He tightened his grip on the steering wheel and pressed down on the accelerator. The truck shot out as he cut through the cars on the freeway.

He was a good ninety minutes away from his home. He'd improve on that estimate by quite a margin if he kept up this speed.

What do they really want? Is it about the kid?

He didn't think so. If his instincts were right, what they wanted was to ruin Cat. Plain and simple.

Did she realize this? If she did, then why wasn't she already in battle mode? And if she didn't realize it, then she was being naïve if she thought she could negotiate with these people.

So, how could he help when the problem was steeped in darkness and secrets? He didn't know.

The car gave him a warning. With the added speed, he was going to run out of juice sooner than expected. Frustrated, he followed the car's directions to a supercharging station to give her enough mileage until he got back to his house.

Once he plugged in his truck, he noticed the deli on the property. The beauty of charging stations was that sustenance was conveniently located in the same area.

He sat at the table and ordered a club sandwich and an Arnold Palmer. He studied the framed newspaper articles on the wall. They reminded him of the clippings that someone had conveniently left for him a few days earlier.

What type of jerks did that?

The evil type. That's what the Rocas were.

He pulled out his phone. The reflection of his face on the glass screen gave him pause. He ran his hand over his facial hair. It was time to shave, to reset and move forward.

He quickly scrolled through the various messages, deleting many, filing some, forwarding others, until he saw one he was not expecting.

An email from Aram Dersch, his first true believer. The Silicon Valley billionaire who had invested in Leo when he was just a teenager.

The subject read *A New Opportunity.*

Curious, he opened the email and read the details. With each sentence, he became more intrigued. Not with what was written, but what wasn't. The email was full of Valley language that implied only one thing—big money ready to invest in a big project.

He replied, *When and where do you want to meet?*

Seconds later, a reply came. *How about now? NDA incoming.*

Leo took a sip of his double espresso as he processed the implications of Aram Dersch's proposal. Aram must've realized that by having lunch at Coupa Café in Palo Alto, a buzz would break out in the Silicon Valley community.

This was a calculated move. As one of five primary investors, Aram wanted the market to get excited about a new potential venture. Based on what Leo had heard, there was plenty to get excited about.

"Thoughts?" Aram asked.

Aram seemed to have aged faster than the decade that had passed since they first met. His receding hairline was in a sprint toward the crown of his head, the salt and pepper Don Quixote goatee was now all salt, and the blue of his eyes was losing its luster. But his mind was sharper than ever.

Leo set his cup down and leaned in a bit. "Are the Pentagon and NASA definitely in?"

Aram shrugged. "As close to a guarantee as we can get with the federal government. This is where we have to be very careful and guarded. In full transparency, Congress killed this project just over a year ago."

Leo flinched. "Say again?"

He didn't like getting involved in political battles.

Aram nodded. "Dead. But the November midterms are just three months away. The new Congress will tip the other way. It's practically a guarantee. But what we can't do is anything that would expose us before our time. We are on a sprint so that in January, when the balance of power shifts, we can produce a proposal that will blow their minds. All the investors and partners must remain under the radar."

"With the names you've shared—"

"The alleged names," Aram interrupted. "We can't share any names."

"Right. With the alleged names you've shared, how could we remain under the radar?"

"What I mean is nothing political, nothing criminal, nothing questionable, no hints, no speculative talk."

Leo scoffed. "You're worried that the politicians who do criminal and questionable things will pull the funding if we do what they do? Love these guys."

Aram snapped his fingers. "Perfect example. You put something like that on Twitter, and we'll have to deal with months of congressional testimonies. What we also don't want is for the investors to be seen by the public as anti-government conspirators. Some companies involved are public companies. The mess they'd be in is incalculable."

He considered telling Aram that the public would be right to question moving forward with a project that had already been cancelled. But he kept it to himself.

Leo finished his coffee. "You asked for my thoughts," he said. "This is probably the most technically challenging, with the least desirable oversight, and the longest time-horizon initiative I've considered. It would prevent me from following up on any other initiatives for at least the first two or three years because of the sheer enormity of this. And the payday is, at best, speculative."

Aram crossed his arms and leaned back. "I hope you have a list of positives coming soon."

Leo shrugged. "Truth is, to design and build the technology that will go into an interstellar space station is something any self-respecting geek will want to be a part of."

"I never thought of you as a Trekker."

"Underneath the bespoke Zegna suits I wear is a kid who grew up on a steady diet of sci-fi TV shows that made him believe in the impossible."

Aram grinned. "So, is that a yes? The team meets Wednesday, at a nondescript JPL facility in the desert."

Leo knew better than to shake his hands in this well-known establishment for billion-dollar deals.

Instead, he nodded, then whispered, "I'm in for phase zero."

Chapter Six

Anna

Anna studied Cat's new trailer. It was perfect. Two bedrooms, a kitchenette, a master bath, and a guest bath. Just what a family needed. All this in less than forty-eight hours. Money sure did open nonexistent doors.

She glanced at her watch. Cat had been out for just over an hour for a meeting with the social worker, or something like that. Cat's belongings, which had been spread between Anna's RV and the onsite storage container, were now being moved to her new place.

Cat could finally have her privacy. If she was being honest, Anna also needed her private space. Meeting at the park with Van was good, but not great. They needed to meet more regularly, and Anna didn't want Cat to worry about what they were doing in secret.

The facility guys from work were nearly finished when Van showed up, and unceremoniously pulled boxes out of his car, and moved them into Anna's RV.

Good morning to you, too.

He was an odd one, but based on the work so far, he was real good at what he did. She frowned when he pulled out oversized flat boxes from the back seat. These were the types of boxes that housed paintings or large frames. She hoped he wasn't going to decorate the place.

"Anna," Van called out. "Join me in the war room."

He disappeared into the RV.

She wanted to remind him that this was her temporary home, not some military compound. But truthfully, she liked that name for her RV. She'd give him a pass on that one.

She entered the RV and immediately understood what those boxes contained. He had taken over one side of the RV and had created an evidence wall.

Four corkboard panels hung on the wall. She hoped for his sake that he had not nailed them to the panels. Unlike Cat's, this RV was rented. On the cork boards were pictures of key players, companies, and their interrelation.

She faced the board. Dead center was Chicho. Connected to him with red twine were Adela Roca, Catalina Alonzo, Rafael Marceli, Elizabeta Marceli, Roberto Chaparral, and others like Lionel, Cat, and some names that she did not recognize.

"I don't want visitors to see this," Anna said.

He faced her, then winked. "I've got that covered."

He pulled out panels that were the same color as the RV's walls and hung them on the corkboards.

"Very slick and very literal," she said. "Now, I've seen these on TV shows. Is it basically interconnections?"

Van crossed his arms, studying the board. "Some call it the Crazy Wall. I don't like that term. It's where investigators pin clues, details, timelines, and connections related to a crime."

She faced him. "Crime?"

He pulled off his sunglasses and slid them onto his shirt. He took out a cigarette and placed it between his lips. "Yeah, definitely a crime."

Where was he going with this? Up to this point, he had not mentioned any findings that would reach that conclusion.

"What crime are we talking about?"

"Not sure. Haven't found it yet, but isn't that why I'm here? There is a suspicion. There is a gut instinct that something is wrong." He faced her. "You asked me to report to you. Why? Because you suspect something."

"Suspicion does not equal crime."

"Not always. But sometimes suspicion leads to much more than just a crime. Sometimes, what we find is downright evil."

Chapter Seven

Catalina

Cat reached the café a few minutes before 9:00 a.m. She took a cleansing breath to regulate her anxiety. She thought making that call was hard. Actually showing up activated a completely different level of fear.

When she was told that Adela would see her, but not at the house, she was initially saddened because she had hoped that she'd see Chicho. Now, in retrospect, as much as she wanted to see her precious boy, she liked the thought of a neutral setting.

Also, if she was being honest, she never wanted to step foot into that home again.

Now, as she approached the front door, Cat wondered why Adela wanted to be seen with her in a public setting. Nothing the Rocas did was random. Everything was calculated.

She pulled the door open, and the aromatic scents of different teas, freshly brewed coffee, and warm pastries filled her senses. As her eyes adjusted from the bright outdoor sunlight to the dimly lit establishment, she saw what she wasn't expecting.

In the middle, at a small circular table, were Adela and her daughter,

Elizabeta. Cat had not seen Elizabeta, her mother-in-law for months. She hesitated at the door, waiting for either one of them to acknowledge her. They didn't.

She scanned the room and saw another odd detail. No one else was here. How was it possible that at nine in the morning, no one else was at the café for breakfast or coffee or a pastry?

"Hi, Cat." A low voice snapped her out of her trance.

It was Barb, the waitress. She looked nervous. Maybe even worried.

"They're waiting for you." She gestured toward the table.

Cat took a deep breath and walked toward them. Five shaky steps and she was next to them. But there was no chair for her.

"Let me get you a chair," Barb said in a hushed tone.

"That won't be necessary," Elizabeta said.

Still no eye contact.

Barb shriveled away and disappeared into the back.

Elizabeta picked up the last of her croissant and plopped it into her mouth. Adela raised her teacup and sipped it.

Finally, Adela faced her. "I don't think our conversation will last long," she said.

Her hair and makeup were perfect. Almost unreal. As if created by an artist and a sculptor.

As for Elizabeta, she had not changed. Sure, strong, dangerous and the looks that would easily disarm anyone.

Cat swallowed, and grabbed a chair from a nearby table, and scraped it along the floor, placing it right by them. She lowered herself while maintaining eye contact with Adela. She would not let them intimidate her. Even though she could barely breathe.

"No, not long," Cat said.

Elizabeta spun to her. "What do you want?"

"Now, now, Eliz," Adela said. "We will hear her out."

They both stared at her. Elizabeta's hate-filled eyes left nothing to the imagination. She didn't want Cat dead. No. That would be too easy. She wanted Cat to suffer.

Adela, on the other hand, wore a low-grade sneer. She also hated Cat. But to her, Cat was slime. A mistake that had caused their family harm.

"Go on," Adela said. "What did you want to discuss?"

Cat swallowed. "I want to bring Chicho—Fransisco—back home. He belongs with me."

Adela scoffed. "You believe that my great grandson belongs with you," she stated. "Let's make sure I understand this, because in my advancing age, things are sometimes harder to process and comprehend." She picked up her napkin and made a show of dabbing her lips. "You believe Francisco should be with the person who is the prime suspect in the murder of the child's father? Furthermore, Francisco should be with the person whose negligence nearly caused the child's death in a fire? Do I have the basic premise of your 'want' captured correctly?"

She sipped her tea again.

Cat's heart rate sped up with each word. Her chest was about to explode, and the rush of blood and thrumming heartbeat muted the sound of everything around her.

This was a mistake.

"That's not what happened," Cat said, but her voice barely came out.

This family—these two in particular—knew how to manipulate her emotions. But she had to try.

"No?" Adela said, in a near musical tone. "Please, educate us."

"It was an accident," Cat said.

"Both incidents were an accident?" Elizabeta asked. "My son dies—no, drowns—and that was a what? Oh, that's right, an accident. And my grandson nearly dies in a—let me guess—accidental fire. Catalina, maybe you are the cause of those accidents. Maybe we're the good guys here. Maybe we're trying to save my grandson, my only living heir, before there's one more premature Marceli headstone added in the cemetery."

Elizabeta's perfectly square jaw pulsated. Her light-brown eyes had slivers of red, like an explosive fire in them. If Cat didn't know any better, this woman would be willing to attack Cat right here and now.

But that was not the Roca or Marceli style. No, they sent people to do their dirty work.

Cat collected herself. "I am here because I want us to find a way for us to work together. For Francisco's sake. He shouldn't have to go through this type of trauma. If you had seen how he cried when they took him—"

"You should've seen how he was laughing this morning," Adela said. "I don't believe this child has had an opportunity to experience the life that he was meant to be born into. He is very happy. Happier than he's ever been."

Cat swallowed and attempted to control the tears that were threatening to burst. She would not cry. Not in front of them. She would not give them the satisfaction.

"I am certain he is happy. And now that I can provide, he will be just as happy—happier with me. Because every child should be with his mother."

Elizabeta exploded to her feet and slammed the table, rattling all the plates.

Cat instinctively scraped her chair back a few inches.

At that same instant, four men appeared, surrounding the table. She knew them and the pieces they carried all in the name of security.

Cat blinked, but did not dare move.

"Yes," Elizabeta said, her voice nearly possessed. "Every child should be with his mother. But you saw to it that I would never have my son with me."

In that moment, Cat understood. She had miscalculated their hatred for her. They would never willingly give up or relinquish Chicho.

"Show her to the door," Adela said.

The men shuffled close, nearly eliminating all the light and air in the room.

She rose before they could touch her. On unsure legs, she turned, then stumbled out the café. She closed the door and picked up her pace, crossing the street and turning the corner. Once out of sight, she leaned against the wall of the pawnshop, then slid down to the ground.

She breathed for the first time since Elizabeta's eruption. A tear slid down her cheek, and she shook.

Cat closed her eyes, took a few deep breaths, then, after a few moments, opened them once again. Nearly a dozen people were staring at her.

She moderated her breathing, quickly wiped the tears, then rose to her feet. She would not make a spectacle of herself. This was what the Rocas wanted. They wanted to break her.

But she was not the same person who lived with them during those abusive days. And just like Elizabeta, Cat also had molten anger. She was a mother, too.

And one way or another, she'd make sure her child came back home.

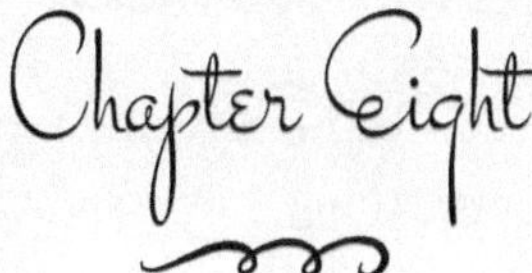

Chapter Eight

Leo

Leo and Chris hustled into the car that would take them to the Van Nuys Airport in the San Fernando Valley. Leo's private jet waited for them to head back to San José.

Leo slid into his seat, then leaned back, eyes closed. He wanted a few seconds to reset, but felt eyes on him. He blinked his open, then faced Chris. He was already staring at Leo; the biggest smile greeted him.

"This. Is. Awesome!"

Leo laughed. He knew Chris would love this.

"We can't mess this one up," Leo said.

"Agreed. We need to white-glove this one. No mistakes, no chances taken. This is one of those once-in-a-lifetime opportunities."

"Once in a generation," Leo corrected. "Time to assemble the team. Let's recruit the best of the best. Steal from others, if we must. We need true disrupters in this space."

Chris grabbed a bottle of beer from the limousine's bar and twisted the cap off. "We need a futurist's view."

Leo loosened his tie. "We need to think beyond the limitations of how we interact with data. The amount of data that this mission will collect means we need to get into full-body gestures—eyes, hands, movements. The astronauts and scientists will need to look and interact with the data in ways that only science fiction has considered."

They both went silent. Leo had been friends with Chris for well over a decade. He could almost read his mind. They made a great team.

"When will Anna be able to join us to get everything organized and launched?" Chris asked.

Leo winced. It was true—he needed Anna, but he would not pull her from helping Cat until everything was squared away. This project, this venture, was amazing.

But Cat was family. The call was his, and the call was an easy one to make. He would take care of this while Anna was helping there.

As is, he felt guilty that he could not be there for Cat. But she was in good hands with Anna and Van.

He knew she understood.

He really hoped she understood.

Once back in his San José office, Leo called Cat. She answered on the third ring.

"Hey," she said. "Hold on a sec."

He could hear the flipping of pages and then the sound of typing on a keyboard.

"Sorry about that," she said. "Was working on something. Let me switch to camera mode."

He set his phone on a small stand on his desk. Her face materialized, and he couldn't help but smile.

"How are you?" she asked.

"I'm good. Wanted to see how you're doing and apologize that I haven't been able to come back."

"You're fine. I've been busy myself. Getting ready for the hearing and other things."

He wanted to kick himself. He didn't even know the hearing's date.

"What's the plan?" he asked.

"For the first hearing, I've asked Chaparral to be with me. But that's just to make sure that nothing obvious is dropped. He won't be the person. He's a safe face for the Rocas to see."

That sounded reasonable, he guessed, although he didn't fully trust him. "And after that?"

"I've been looking at options that Anna has sent me, but last night I woke up from a dream where I saw your dad's other attorney in it."

"Maroutian?"

"Yup."

"From a dream?" He didn't mean to sound confused. He just was confused.

"Hear me out." She sounded excited, full of energy. "Your dad trusted him. If I know anything about Lionel, it's that he trusted with sincere frugality."

"Truer words have never been spoken," Leo said. His dad was very slow to trust, so maybe she was onto something. "Have you spoken to him?"

"Not yet. Spoke to Anna about it, and she told me she'll be paying him a visit soon. I asked her to assess him, like on an instinctual level, when she's there."

Leo liked where she was going with this. And he linked that she'd stopped the whole 'I need time' business. Because there was no time to waste. "Anna is great at reading people. But I suspect he doesn't do family law. These guys usually specialize."

"Even if he doesn't, I would trust him to refer someone who is trustworthy. So I'm just rolling with the possibility that I saw him in my dream for a reason." She actually smiled.

He was not one to diminish the value of dreams. Some of his favorite solutions had appeared in a dream first.

"Love it. Glad that's progressing well. How's everything else? Have you seen Chicho yet?" he asked.

Her smile faltered, and he wanted to shove the largest shoe he could find into his mouth.

"No. Not yet. We'll see what they say at the hearing. I'm praying that the decision will be reversed, and I get him back ASAP. But I suspect I have my work cut out with the Rocas."

He nodded. "I suspect you're right."

She seemed to lean into the camera.

"Is that your office?" she asked.

He nodded. "Yup."

"Wow. It almost looks impressive. Give me a tour."

He plucked the phone off the stand and flipped the camera's direction. "This is me," he said, panning the camera around.

"Yikes! That's your view? It's amazing."

She was right. He had a nice place with a great view.

He tapped the phone, pointing the camera back to his face. "Once things have been resolved, and my crazy schedule improves, I'll bring you guys up here so you can see the place."

She smiled and nodded. "I'd love that."

He missed her. Even though it had only been a few days, he wanted to see her again. But this was a bad time with all that was happening with the Pentagon and NASA.

"What are you working on?" she asked. "Can you tell me about it?"

He shrugged. "Not yet. And definitely not on the phone. But it is truly an epic opportunity. It's one of those initiatives where we were forced to sign away our firstborn if we broke the NDA."

"Oh, so you're planning to have a firstborn? That's breaking news."

He hesitated. But then he realized he wanted to be a dad at some point. "Well, yeah. The Moncrieff name must continue. And I must do my part to help with the depopulation crisis."

She grinned. "I bet you will. You'll be a wonderful dad."

He had never even thought about that. A dad. Him. Hard to even imagine it.

"Speaking of dads," she said, snapping him out of his thoughts. "I hope you don't mind, but I took your dad's journal to see if I can make heads or tails out of it. Since we still don't know what his secret project may have been, this seems like the most obvious place to start. I'm digging into some things around here, and I feel like your dad's book may hold some answers."

He studied her. She had always been one of those research geeks when they were in high school. He should've been the one doing the research, but he was too tied up right now.

"That sounds amazing. Let me know if you need anything."

She seemed to consider something. "Do you guys have a laptop that's better than your dad's late 90s desktop that I could borrow?"

"You'll have it tomorrow morning," he said.

She smiled. "Now only if I could get you to show up that easily."

His heart broke at that moment. He wanted to see her, too. But. There was always a but.

"Soon enough," he said, not knowing if he was telling her the truth.

"Soon enough," she echoed.

Chapter Nine

Anna

Anna and Van waited in Ricardo Chaparral's law office's waiting room. This man seemed to be at the center of everything. Not that he was the one orchestrating things, but he was literally the person who had been in between Cat, Lionel, the realtors, the fire insurance, and so on. Interestingly, he had not been the one responsible for the execution of the will.

"Mister Chaparral will see you now," his assistant said.

Anna rose, but Van remained seated. She glanced at him. His eyes had frozen on nothing in particular. He was far, far away.

"Van," she said as she touched his shoulder.

He snapped to. "Sorry," he mumbled as he rose.

Ricardo opened the door. "This is a pleasant surprise," he said, not completely sounding like he believed it.

They all sat around the conference table.

Ricardo studied Van for a moment, then turned to Anna. "So, what brings you here?"

"We're working on several fronts to help Cat. This is Van, Leo's friend. He's been helping us."

"Van..." Ricardo repeated, almost to himself. His eyes widened. "Oh, that's right. You were looking into Lionel's medical records."

"That's right," Van said. "Still working on it."

"So, you're a private investigator?"

"I am."

Anna studied the interaction. Ricardo's body language had gone into defensive mode. Van, on the other hand, remained cool and collected. Almost like he was reading Ricardo's mind one neuron at a time.

"Now I'm really intrigued about this visit," Ricardo said. "So, how can I help?"

"First, we need some historical context. How did the Rocas become such an influential family here?" Van asked.

Ricardo leaned back. "Wow. That story goes back to decades ago. But in the simplest terms, they were one of the original families who migrated here from Spain over a century ago."

"Along with the Casa family?" Van added.

"Yes, that's right. Leo's maternal side was the first. But within a few years, the Roca family had also migrated here. The Rocas established this little harbor town. They were the leaders of the fishing industry here. They invested wisely and, over time, bought more of the land in the area. I don't think you'll find a plot of land or a business that the Roca family has not touched at some point or another."

"Including yours?" Van asked.

Involuntarily, Anna's eyes widened.

Ricardo fidgeted in his seat.

"What I mean," Van said, "is that most likely this office building is owned by the Rocas. So you lease from them."

"Well...yes. Not them directly, though. One of their many businesses in the area."

Van nodded and made a note in his tiny notebook. "But their empire seems to go beyond the borders of this town."

Ricardo rubbed his forehead. "Yes, they do. But I wouldn't call it an empire." He shifted in his chair again. "I'm sorry, but how is this relevant to Catalina and Francisco's situation?"

Anna stepped in. "To put it bluntly, Cat doesn't have too many friends here. Excluding you, of course."

He eased. "Well, yes. I have always made myself available to her."

"And if the town is somehow compromised because they don't want to go against their benefactor, then it begs the question—how can Cat get fair treatment here?"

Ricardo shook his head. "I don't think that's an issue. We all have someone or some company that we have to pay for our home, our cars, our businesses. It's a business transaction. What Cat is going against is a family who are respected and admired."

"Admired?" Van asked.

"Yes, admired. They do a lot for this town. All improvements are through them. And amid tragedy, they've been able to overcome it."

"The tragedy being the death of Rafael Marceli," Van said.

"Yes, that was a very difficult period for many of us. We'd seen him grow up here. He was... He was..."

"What was he?" Anna asked.

"Everyone knew him," Ricardo said. "No one wants to see one of their own die."

"Interesting," Van said, nearly to himself.

"Why do you find that interesting?" Ricardo asked Van.

"Cat was born and raised here also. They all saw her grow up here, but they don't seem to support her."

Ricardo studied Van for a long moment. "No, I suppose not."

"Why did everyone assume she was behind Rafael Marceli's death?" Anna asked.

"Isn't that typical?" Ricardo answered.

"Yes, but this isn't a typical town, is it? He goes off boating during a storm. Why assume it was her?"

Ricardo went silent.

Van continued. "Typically, the reason law enforcement suspects the spouse is because there is some history. Was there history?"

Ricardo crossed his arms. "I wouldn't know anything about that."

"And yet, the police went after her first. They didn't chalk it off to a tragic accident," Van said. "Even when they found the body, there was no sign of foul play. At least not according to the court records."

"Like I said," Ricardo said, "I wouldn't know anything about that." He looked at his watch. "My apologies, but I have another appointment coming up. If that will be all..."

He rose.

"You've been very generous with your time," Anna said as they all rose. "We may have some follow-ups."

"I probably won't be of much use, but if I can—"

"Actually, another question," Van said as they walked into the reception area. "Why did Lionel Sr. choose an outside attorney to represent his will and be his executor?"

"Well...he probably didn't want our friendship to get in the way," Ricardo said.

"You're probably right," Van said. As they got to the door, he turned one more time. "I'm curious. Who was the executor on his original will?"

"Original?"

"Yes, because as I understood it, everyone, including you, was surprised that the new attorney was involved. So, who was in the original version?"

Silence joined them. Anna watched Ricardo's unblinking eyes. He finally smiled.

"The version from 2010 had me listed as his executor," Ricardo said.

"Interesting," Van said, then looked around the empty reception area. "Your next appointment is late. We'll get out of your hair. Thanks again."

They shook hands, their eyes locked.

"Thank you," Anna said, breaking the stare down.

Ricardo turned and offered her a hand as well. "Until next time," he said, then spun away and went to his office.

Van calmly walked down the stairs, and Anna followed him. She could feel the strain of the smile that pulled at her lips.

Once outside, she tapped his shoulder. He turned as he slid on his sunglasses.

"What do you think?" she asked.

"More digging required. But this Chaparral character... Not loving him," Van said.

She studied Van's face. He was right about Chaparral. More importantly, she had been wrong about Van.

This man was good. Really good.

Back in the RV, Van added a note to the crime board.

"We know that Leo's dad didn't trust Chaparral," Van said.

"At one point he did. So what changed?" Anna asked.

"Cat, that's what. Up to that point, the home would go to his son. But once he gifted the home to Cat, he knew he had changed the equation. Word would get out. The wrong people would find out."

"You're saying Ricardo would tell the Rocas?"

He glanced at her. "I don't know. I'm making connections. Why introduce Maroutian as an impartial attorney into this? He must have zero overlap with the influential web of the Roca family. Leo's dad must've known that."

Anna sat on the sofa. "This doesn't mean Lionel thought Ricardo was crooked. Maybe Lionel didn't want his new plan to be mentioned, even innocently, by Ricardo to others—like his secretary. It could be an innocent decision."

Van leaned into the table and studied her. He trained his eyes directly on hers. She would not be the first to break eye contact.

"Do you always assume the best in people?"

She scoffed. "No, not always. But small towns have a tendency to have a rumor mill. Sometimes vicious ones that can spread horrible rumors. This one has the makings of one of those types."

He glanced at her again. "Vicious rumor mills, you say? You sound like you speak from experience."

She smiled. "Maybe I do."

He winked at her. "Maybe you do."

Chapter Ten

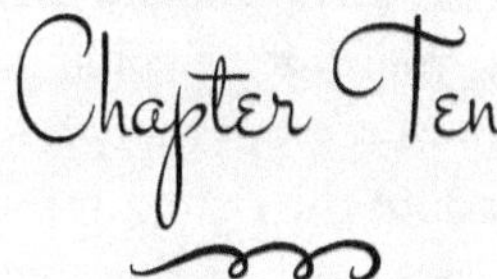

Catalina

The sounds of tapping feet and shuffling papers echoed throughout the courtroom.

Cat took a deep breath, then drank from her water bottle, checked to make sure her top was buttoned properly, then ran her fingers through her hair. She wanted to look perfect for when the judge walked in.

Thankfully, neither Elizabeta nor Adela were in court.

Someone laid a hand on her shoulder and squeezed. Lola and Anna were there waiting to hear the judge's ruling on this first phase. Van hung out at the back of the courtroom.

Leo had not come. She'd told Leo that he did not have to. But now that she was here, she wished he had. She needed her entire team with her.

Today was Lola's last day in Fortuny Bay before she had to head back to her place at Pismo Beach. Lola's ordinary life was about to start. While Cat's ordinary was anything but.

"You okay, Sis?"

"Livin' the dream," Cat said.

All three grinned, but the smiles did not last.

"Here comes the bailiff," Roberto whispered.

They all rose. The bailiff said something, and Judge McAuliffe walked in. Words were said, but she could barely hear any of that.

Her heart was in her throat. She could barely breathe. Five days ago, this court had approved the removal of her son from her car. She hoped today they'd issue a reversal.

"Anything is possible," Roberto had said the day before. "He could just hand over custody back to you. But he could go the exact opposite direction, too. The court's foremost responsibility is to the child."

Cat knew Roberto was not the right attorney for this matter. But the judge knew him, he was respected in the community, and his presence would not be seen as a shot across the Roca bow. That was her goal.

She snapped out of her thoughts. The judge continued to ramble.

"Child Protective Services is necessary, but it is never ideal for a child to be in their care or under the care of an appointed family. Not when this court had previously established an alternative. I understand the child has been with his grandmother, Elizabeta Marceli," the judge said.

"Yes, Your Honor," the other side's attorney said.

The judge flipped through some papers on his desk. "Let's see... Miss Catalina Marceli had partial custody for the last three months under specific court-appointed limitations. However, after the fire incident at Miss Catalina Marceli's residence, and based on the initial fire report, partial custody was suspended and guardianship over Francisco was transferred back to the Marceli family. Is that accurate?"

He looked from one attorney to the other.

"Yes, Your Honor," Roberto said.

The other side also concurred.

"Very well. Therefore, until we have clarity over the incident and we have CPS's recommendation, it is the decision of this court that in the interim, full custody be given to the grandparent, Elizabeta Marceli."

Out of Cat's throat, a sound escaped.

"Be calm," Roberto whispered, and squeezed her arm. He leaned in. "He's better off with them than being with a foster family."

Was he? She wasn't sure about that.

The judge turned to her and lowered his glasses to the tip of his nose. "As I said, this is temporary until we see more from you, Miss Marceli. Every court wants a child to be with their biological parents. Until the next time this court convenes, I want to see progress from you and I suggest you listen to Roberto."

Movement came from the Roca side of the court.

"But no court will ever place a child in the hands of a negligent or a dangerous parent."

"Yes, Your Honor," she said.

"Supervised visitation under the guidance of CPS is approved," the judge said.

He explained the conditions, but once again, the sounds in the courtroom were replaced by her heartbeat. She felt numb.

The judge said a few more things that she didn't quite hear. The gavel struck the sound block, and everyone collected their things and rose.

Cat turned to Roberto. "So...what happens next? I'm sorry, I'm just a bit..."

Anna and Lola joined them.

"The social worker is expecting you today. Give her reasons to have confidence in you. What CPS says has a lot of weight for the court."

"You've met with the social worker before, right?" Lola asked.

"Yes, I have. She's decent. She seemed to care for Chicho."

"Even so," Anna said. "I think you have to be prudent with everyone involved."

There was something that Anna was not saying. Or at least implying. Maybe she was right. Maybe she needed to be careful with who she trusted.

"Most importantly," Roberto said. "You'll get to see Francisco today."

She smiled. "Finally."

Van volunteered to take Cat to the CPS office. No words were exchanged during the drive. Mostly because Van played 80s music through the one functioning speaker in his car. He had a cable connecting from his very modern phone to what he called a cassette deck.

She took a quick look at him. He couldn't have been a hair over thirty. Silver aviator sunglasses fully covered his eyes, so even when he spoke to her, she wasn't sure if he was addressing her.

"So, you work for Anna?" she asked.

"You could say that."

That was an odd response. "Do you work at the same company?"

"No. Nothing like that. I'm a private contractor."

"Like a consultant?" she asked.

"You could say that." He was certainly no master conversationalist.

"Would *you* say that?" she asked and waited.

He turned to her, and an actual grin parted his mouth. "Yeah, I'd say that."

She was very proud of herself. She had gotten him to finally engage with her.

"Here we are," he said as they pulled in front of the building.

She took a deep breath. "Wish me luck," she said as she opened her door.

"I'll be right here."

"You don't have to do that. This may take a while. I can call when I'm done."

"I'll be right here. Add me to your contacts."

She did.

"If you need anything, just text me," he said.

There was something in his tone that gave her the impression that he wasn't talking about coffee runs.

"I will."

Before she could step out, three large, heavily tinted, black Escalades pulled up.

"That's them," she whispered.

The doors opened, and large men in dark suits rushed out. For just an instant, she thought she saw a little body in between them. She would not have to guess or wonder. She would see her son.

"If you need anything, just text me," Van repeated.

She eyed him. Now she understood what he really meant.

Cat focused on her breathing. She knew that anxiety was not what Maggie Ostensen would want to see from Cat. The social worker seemed decent enough, but decency was not the game they played.

Cat understood that there was a lot of abuse in the world. She knew it firsthand. She just had to show Maggie that she really was the good one in this situation.

Cat had walked into the office with confidence, ready to have the talk, ready to show Maggie that Chicho would be safe. Beyond that, she would show Maggie that he needed to be with his mother—not this family who used intimidation the way most people breathed.

But her confidence was faltering now. She'd been waiting for just over twenty minutes.

"Hello, Catalina," a voice called out.

Cat looked up and saw Maggie walking toward her.

Cat quickly rose to her feet, causing her phone to leap off her lap and slam into the linoleum floor.

"Oh no," Maggie said as she approached the phone. "Didn't mean to startle you."

She couldn't show Maggie that she was nervous or worried. "No, no. You didn't startle me," she said as they both reached the phone, but Maggie picked it up first.

"The screen cracked," Maggie said.

"It was already broken," Cat said.

Maggie gave her a sympathetic smile.

Why did I say that?

Now, Maggie would think that Cat was irresponsible and content to live with broken things. How could someone who couldn't take care of or repair a phone be able to take care of a child?

Stop overthinking everything!

"Let's go to the conference room," Maggie said.

Cat followed her. With each step, she felt her breathing shorten.

Calm down, Cat!

"Take a seat," Maggie said.

Lord help me.

Three simple words, and in that moment, warmth enveloped her. A hint of calm entered her heart. Not overwhelming, and not complete calm, but just enough.

"How are you?" Maggie asked.

Her dark-green eyes against the backdrop of her pixie cut red hair made her look like an ancient elf.

"I haven't seen my son for five days. So, I'm not well."

She nodded. "That's understandable, clearly. CPS is committed to family reunification if possible. But there is a process to these things—as you know."

"Look, I'm just glad that I get to see him today. The rest we'll work out. I'm sure of it."

Maggie studied her. "As you can imagine, the Marceli and Roca families are fighting this."

Cat shifted in her seat.

"However, what people want is not our concern," Maggie said. "CPS needs to know that his home with you is safe. Based on our finding, we will provide the court our recommendation."

"But I don't really understand how we got here. What happened with the fire is not something I could've controlled. So why are we being punished for an uncontrollable incident?"

Maggie leaned back. "The house was not safe, per the fire inspector. The fire could've been avoided."

This was news. She had not heard any details so far.

"How is that neglect?" Cat asked.

"Imagine you own a car. Imagine your child sits in that car. Now imagine that there's a leak in the muffler or the gas tank, and the fumes enter the car's cabin. It's not your fault that the car has the problem—you didn't cause the leak. But it is your responsibility to address that leak. Especially when you're already on a very short..."

"Leash?"

Maggie bit the inside of her lip, looked over her shoulder, then leaned in. "Get your house and affairs in order. Show the court that you're the right place for Francisco. The court needs to see this. I suspect the fire inspector's final report will clear you of negligence. The houses in Fortuny Bay are old. Very old. That's one. You also need to show that you have the means to support your family. You will need to get a job."

Cat blinked. How was she supposed to even think about of finding a job when all this was going on? But she checked herself and found the words she needed to use. "Well, to be honest, my focus has been on getting Chicho back, getting our temporary home into a comfortable, safe space for us, and then after that, it was going to be the rebuilding of the home."

Maggie pushed her glasses up the bridge of her nose. "I see." She leaned in. "I realize that you have money right now, but money runs out. Over seventy percent of lottery winners go bankrupt in less than five years. That also applies to inheritances. The court does not look at a savings account as viable, particularly when...when it was gifted to you. They may see it as a ploy, and therefore not sustainable, or possibly even temporary."

Cat blinked. "I can't even... I don't know who would hire me right now. Particularly in town. My late husband stopped me from getting my degree, so I don't have a marketable skill."

Maggie frowned. "There are always options. There are even remote jobs these days. Don't give the court a reason to hesitate." She paused. "Do you understand me?"

"I do," Cat said.

"Good. Now, sit and relax. I'll get Francisco."

Cat paced around the conference room. She was certain she was about to puke.

The door opened.

Maggie stepped in. Holding the hand of the most beautiful sight she'd ever seen.

"Momma!" Chicho yelled and ran full steam into her embrace. She lifted him off the floor and spun him around and around.

She cried. He cried. She kissed his cheek over and over again. She laughed. He laughed.

She set him back down and pulled back. "Let me look at you," she said. "Is that a beard you're growing?"

He laughed. "No, Mom. I'm a kid still."

She pulled him in again for a hug. "I missed you," she whispered.

"I missed you, too," he said.

"Let's sit on the couch," Maggie said, pulling them both out of the moment of euphoria.

This was a temporary reunion. Her time was limited.

"Are you eating well?" she asked, just as they sat next to each other. Maggie sat on a chair facing them.

"Yeah, I'm eating all the time. Grandma has a restaurant in her house," he said.

Grandma. That nearly broke her heart.

"A restaurant? I don't remember that."

"It's true. I say what I want, and it shows up. I say hamburger. I get it. I say pizza or ice cream. I get it all. And it tastes so yummy."

"I bet." She combed his hair. "It's getting a little long."

"I don't want to cut it. I want to grow it out."

"Really, why?"

He shrugged. "Just want to."

"You'll look very handsome, I'm sure." She pulled out her phone. "Check this out," she said and was about to give it to Chicho, but Maggie stopped her.

"Let me see it first, please," Maggie said.

What did Maggie think she'd show her son? A warning message? But she didn't argue.

Instead, she handed over phone and said, "Of course."

Maggie flipped through her pictures and then returned her the phone. "Go ahead."

"What is it, Mom?"

She showed him pictures of the trailer.

His eyes grew wide with excitement. "Is that one my room?"

"It sure is."

"When can I go?"

Cat looked at Maggie.

"Not yet, Francisco," Maggie said. "We talked about this, right?"

He nodded, but he did not look satisfied. "How about the big house? Is it fixed now?"

"Soon. It'll be amazing and beautiful."

He smiled, then hugged her. "I miss you, Mom." He started crying. "I miss Lola. I miss Anna. And I miss Leo a lot. I want to be back home."

Cat couldn't speak. Any attempt would release the dam of emotions that she was holding back.

"Soon enough," Maggie said.

She prayed Maggie was right. This was torture.

Chapter Eleven

Leo

Leo didn't want to be one of *those* people. But he'd been waiting for a play-by-play from Cat for hours now. He wasn't sure, but he thought by the time she saw her phone, she'd see a dozen missed calls.

He should've gone to the hearing. Not that he could've, since things were heating up with the project. But still. That would've been the right thing to do.

The last phone conversation with Cat still rang in Leo's ears. Something was happening between them, and as difficult as it was to admit, he loved hearing her voice.

But what had him a bit off was a simple fact—he missed her. He wanted to talk to her every day, all day. Clearly, that was ridiculous. No one —and he meant no one—had that type of effect on him.

Sometimes, projects had him in that obsessive state. But this wasn't about being obsessive. He would not dare put into words what he thought was going on.

His phone rang. It was Cat.

"Finally," he said as he answered the video call.

Her beautiful face filled the screen.

"Hey, you. What a day," she said as she ran her hand through her hair. "Where do I start?"

"How's Chicho?"

Her eyes glistened. "He's lovelier than ever. He asked about you. And your spaceship."

Something tweaked in his heart. A stinging sensation caused his eyes to practically burn. He swallowed and controlled himself.

She quickly brought him up to date on the court's ruling and the next steps.

"When do you see Chicho next?"

"Next week. It's seriously killing me. I feel like a part of me has been ripped out. I feel incomplete without him."

He wished he was there to comfort her. To hold her and give her encouragement. To help her move things along. And to be there as she crosses the finish line.

"I'm sorry I wasn't there for you," he said.

"Don't be. I'm good. I've got an amazing support crew here. Even Van. In his pay-by-the-word way, he is a comfort."

This was insane. He was missing out on the most important thing that was happening to the most important person in his life. "I'll be there soon."

"I know you'll come when you can. You don't need to say much more than that."

After he got off the phone, he had zero interest in looking at his emails or look through the documents that had been sent to him. He missed her and he was worried about her. There was only one thing that could be done. He had to ask his in-house spy how Cat was really doing.

Two rings, and Anna answered.

"I got the links to the private documentation site. I'll get into it tonight," she said.

"Hi, Anna. Good to hear from you, too."

"Seriously? Of all people, you're accusing me of not having proper phone etiquette?"

"Don't even know what you're talking about. I'm very cordial and always interested in my team's well-being above all else."

She laughed. "You keep weaving that story. Go on, then. What did you want?"

"Must I want something? Maybe I'm calling my friend to see how she's doing."

"Oh, I see. You're calling to find out about Cat." She thickened her voice to imitate his. "Maybe I'm calling my friend to see how she's doing," she repeated. "Just ask me straight out, and I'll tell you."

"Fine," he snapped. "How's Cat doing?"

A few seconds ticked by. "Why do you ask? You like her or something?"

"Are you itching for a fight? Is that it? Because I'll come over there and box it out, if that's what you want."

"I'd totally win," she said.

Something in her tone was different. He wondered, but he would not push it over the phone.

He wanted to see her eyes if he was going to quiz her. "Okay, Miss Sunny Disposition, tell me. What's the latest with Cat? With Chicho? With the house?"

"The latest concern is about a conversation she had with the social worker. She needs a job. Bottom line, just because she has money in the bank—a combination of inheritance and a gift from you—does not mean that the court will approve of how she plans to provide. So she's trying to land a job."

"And no one local wants to be on the wrong side of the Rocas."

"Exactly. But she's not giving up."

"So what does that mean about building the house?"

"It means she's gotten zero traction. Between us, the temporary home has removed all urgency. And now, if she has to get a job..."

"With a full-time job, she'll never have the time she needs to get the project off the ground."

"Exactly."

A few ideas popped into his head. "I think I need to get involved."

"Hold on," Anna jumped in. "You're deep with the NASA project."

"Yes, I know. Put me in touch with the builder who Sophie told us about. The guy in Malibu."

"José Díaz. He's a good one. Let me text him while I have you."

While she did that, he looked him up online. The guy had a super impressive portfolio. His specialty was beachfront property, so this would be perfect.

"You're in luck," she said. "He's up in Pismo Beach for some surfing tournament. He can be up here tomorrow."

"He surfs?"

"That's what you got from what I just told you?" Anna asked.

"No, no, it's just that some things create a mental picture, and that one didn't work. Anyway, that's great. Please get him the address to the coffee shop in Fortuny Bay."

"Not here?"

"No," he said. "I want to meet with him first, and we'll drive up together."

"Okay, should I tell Cat?"

"Nope. I want to surprise her." He grinned.

This was a brilliant idea.

Leo barely slept. Whether it was because of the plan that he'd concocted or because after nearly a week, he'd get to see Cat again, he was not sure.

But sleep eluded him, and each time he thought of her, he tempered it because he understood that her primary goal was getting her child back, not rekindling anything with Leo.

José was already at the café when Leo arrived in Fortuny Bay. Over Nutella croissants and coffee, Leo shared his master plan with the builder and was happy to see that José was ready to help.

Twenty minutes later, their two trucks pulled up into Cat's dirt drive.

"Beautiful property," José said once they both got out of their vehicles.

"Twenty acres up to the beach," Leo added.

Just then, Anna exited her RV. She'd picked up a few shades of tanned skin.

"Hello, José," Anna said.

Another door opened and closed.

"Leo?" Cat asked from behind them.

Uncontrollably, he smiled when he saw her. He marched toward her, and she hurried in his direction.

They met in an embrace. He was tempted to lift her off her feet. Instead, he breathed her in and squeezed hard.

"Missed you, Cat," he whispered.

She let go and studied him. Just for that smile alone, he'd take that drive every day. He caught himself in mid-thought.

Check yourself.

She caressed his face. "You shaved."

He just nodded.

"What brings you here?" she asked. "Not that I'm complaining or anything, but you didn't say anything yesterday when we spoke."

"I remember how much you liked surprises."

An eyebrow rose. "You must remember someone else."

He turned and motioned toward José. "This is my friend, José Díaz. He's a builder."

"Nice to meet you," José said as he shook her hand. "This is a very rare type of architecture for this part of the country."

"What do you mean?" she asked.

"She has elements of Cape Cod, which surprisingly works really well with the type of foliage and sand dunes you have here. Do you know who designed it?" he asked as he walked around the structure.

The others followed.

She shook her head. "No clue."

"It would be interesting to know if a known architect designed this. Are you thinking of tearing it down?"

"No. I'd love to restore it back to the way it was," she said.

They stood on the rear porch, which was mostly intact other than some water and smoke damage.

"Maybe with new appliances, better insulation, solid windows, a durable roof," Leo said. "But that's just my opinion."

José nodded. "That's par for the course," he said. "Your builder will have to meet code while preserving the original architecture."

They continued to the north side of the house and waited as José checked some sidings.

Leo faced Cat, who was already studying him.

"So, what brings you two here?" The suspicion in her voice was unmistakable.

"José's a Malibu-based builder. We are talking about a potential project down there. He happened to be in the area. He was...umm...surfing in Pismo." As soon as he said that, he knew he'd messed up.

José laughed. "No, no. I don't surf. My daughter and nephew are the surfers. I was there watching them."

"So you came to Casa Moncrieff to..."

"I figured since he was in the area," Leo said, "he could take an objective look at the structure so that you have a base understanding of what you're dealing with. I don't know what your eventual builder will tell you, but José is a trusted partner."

She nodded, then kicked a piece of stone away. "I still don't have a builder," she said. "So if you know anyone who is willing to work in this area..."

José frowned. "I can ask around."

"If they're local to within fifty miles, I can already tell you they won't take the job. There appears to be a notice above my head advising all local builders to stay away."

Leo's anger inched up a few degrees. This he was not aware of.

"Is that right?" José looked at the house again. "Look, first things first. Let me check it out and see what we're dealing with. Then I can look into reputable builders who would love this type of project."

She tilted her head. "What do you mean by this *type* of project?"

"A restoration of a classic. She's got great bones."

"One other thing worth mentioning," Leo said. "My mom had drawings and ideas on how to expand this home. Would you be able to look at the feasibility of doing that also?"

"Absolutely. I can also have my favorite architect look at it, too."

"Pete Nicos?" Anna asked.

"He's the one. That guy gets it."

"What do you think?" Leo asked Cat.

"Are you kidding me? I'm finally feeling hopeful. But I don't want to get ahead of myself."

"You're right. Let me first gear up and check out the house," José said.

As he walked away, Cat squeezed into Leo's side. He dropped his arm around her shoulder, and she placed her head on his chest. He missed this. This was what he needed.

"So, he just happened to be in the area," she said.

"Amazing luck."

"Indeed," she said. "I could use some of that luck to help me land a job soon."

"Out of curiosity, if you ran a bed-and-breakfast, isn't that a job?" he asked.

"Well... "she said, then straightened. "I suppose. But until that happens, we're talking about what, a year? Maybe more? I need to get Chicho back as soon as possible. Waiting is not an option."

She was right. Waiting while that boy was with that family would not be wise.

Something had to give.

Chapter Twelve

Anna

Van pulled into the dirt driveway. He maneuvered his car around the two trucks and positioned it with the front facing out. He then slid out of the car, closed it, but did not lock it. Never locked. Anna had once asked him why he parked the way he did.

"For fast escape and exit," he'd answered.

He was an intriguing, and potentially paranoid, man.

"Leo," he said.

They exchanged hugs, the type that only men do. A clasped arm in between each, sufficient separation, but close enough that one arm can wrap around the back of the friend and tap it a couple of times. What she called a bro hug—whether correct or not.

"How's it going?" Leo asked.

Van looked around, made eye contact with Anna, and he did that little thing that she understood to mean, "join us."

"Do you have a couple of minutes?" Van asked.

Leo turned toward Cat and saw that she was talking with José, who had just come out from underneath the raised foundation.

"Sure," Leo said to Van.

They all entered Anna's RV and gathered around the table.

"I've been going over the medical records," Van said.

"My dad's?"

"Yes."

"Not sure if you need to do that," Leo said.

"Well," Anna interjected, "we have a larger theory around this town and how they operate."

Leo leaned back and frowned. "Which is...?"

"The working theory is that everything is interconnected and nothing is a coincidence, until proven otherwise," Anna said.

Leo blinked, then sank into his chair. "Go on."

"It's a multi-pronged approach. The battle over Chicho. Your father's health. Rafa's death. The fire. The fire insurance. The fire inspector's report. Your father's journal and missing passion project."

Leo ran a hand through his hair. "And the ship and boat in the middle of the night."

"What ship?" Van asked.

Anna explained what little she knew.

"We need to look at that more carefully," Van said. "Whatever that is, they are right off of the beach that leads into this property."

Leo nodded. "Excellent point. Okay, so I understand the approach. What have you found so far?"

Van opened the crime board panel and showed the spiderweb of connections.

"Wow," Leo breathed out and stood. He studied it for a few moments. "Has Cat seen this?"

"No, not yet," Anna said.

He nodded. "Probably best for now, so that she remains focused on what she has to do. Until we have facts."

"Our thoughts exactly," Anna said. "Now, let's start with your dad's health."

She nodded to Van.

Van closed the crime board. "Here are summaries of your father's medical diagnosis."

He pulled a sheet out from a folder and placed it in front of Leo.

Leo scanned it. One horrible sounding diagnosis after another. Leo pushed the paper away. "I don't know what they mean, but it sounds bad."

"It is," Van said without emotion. "And yes, it can be fatal. However, the most important element should've been addressable. He was losing blood regularly."

"I remember Cat mentioning that," Leo said.

"Per the records, he would feel very weak, in severe pain, and unable to do much. Until he got the transfusion."

"Which in and of itself is what is expected," Anna jumped in. "He was losing blood, so when he was low, his body would go into shutdown mode. It's like running a car with nearly zero oil. Pushing it to the limit, then adding a bit more, pushing, and a bit more. You would come to a point of severe and irreversible breakdown."

"We looked at his meds," Van said. "All appropriate for the diagnosis."

Leo rose. "Then I guess that's that. He had a legitimate condition. His medical treatment was appropriate, and so were his medications."

"Yes," Van said. "However, there are questions."

"Such as?"

"Why wasn't the blood transfusion enough?" Van started. "He was getting two units every two weeks. By all measures, that should've been more than enough. And yet, after one week, he was already low, hurting, and suffering."

"Which means that he was only relatively okay for one week out of two," Anna said. "He suffered during the second week."

She studied Leo's flinch.

"Finally, why couldn't they stop the internal bleeding? They cauterized a few times, but for some reason, he'd suddenly get horrible pain, and once again, he'd have a bleeding ulcer."

Leo sat back down. "Are you thinking medical negligence?"

Van shook his head. "Let's go back to the working theory. Everything is interconnected, and there are no coincidences."

"I'm listening, but I suspect I'm not gonna like where you take this."

"Your dad took in Miss Alonzo," Van said.

"That must've angered the Roca family," Anna added.

"They wanted to even the score," Van said. "An opportunity opened up."

"A legitimate medical concern that should've been addressed, and yet... things got worse," Anna said. "We're going to start with the doctor a little later today, the infusion center, nurses, everything. If we smell anything irregular, then a connection has been made with the Roca approach to solving issues."

Leo's jaw pulsated. She knew he wouldn't like hearing the theory, but he had to know.

"Good work. Any findings in the other areas you mentioned?"

"We're meeting Maroutian tomorrow," Van said. "We're visiting the detective in charge of the Rafael Marceli investigation the next day."

"And the fire?" Leo asked.

"The inspector is on leave," Anna said. "And no one seems to know when he'll be back."

"What does that mean?" Leo asked.

"We don't know," Van said.

"I don't believe any of these things are coincidences," Anna said. "And we have to assume the Rocas are dangerous and willing to use their influence."

Chapter Thirteen

Catalina

Cat closed the lid of her new laptop and tapped her fingers on it. She should've been job hunting, but instead, she was researching.

The Roca empire was far and wide. From the outside, it all looked legitimate. But she knew that the type of money they brought in was not from running a harbor and fishing operations. She could not put her finger on it. But she was determined to find an angle.

And she was certain that Lionel had been close. She glanced at his journal. What did all those entries mean? Maybe she needed to bounce off some ideas with Leo or Anna.

She glanced at her RV. They had all left her alone. They were presumably talking business about the project that he couldn't tell her about. Either way, she was glad he was here. Just knowing that he was within a stone's throw was good enough for her.

She really liked José, and even based on the first pass of information he'd shared, she had updated the master spreadsheet for the planned construction activities. She would not sit idle and do nothing. There were a few construction approaches that she liked.

After a couple of sleepless nights, the new model was finished and had even received a wide-eyed approval from Anna. Before meeting Rafa, Cat had aspirations of getting an MBA. She was supposed to become a leader in industry. Instead, for years, she had a master's in surviving.

She took a deep breath of the coastal air, then glanced at the house. Maybe José would find the team she needed to have a home again. He was inside the house now, going from room to room, evaluating the damage.

At this moment, there was some momentum with the house. But the other matters were still open. The next day, Anna was to meet with Maroutian. She hoped something would come from that, because she needed to get her precious boy back home.

And right now, with a court date looming, she needed to land a job and finalize on a real attorney.

A real attorney also meant that she'd burn through her cash at a faster rate. Which was exactly what the Rocas were counting on. No cash, no fight, game over.

She knew that a more expert lawyer was what she needed, but she supposed having Chaparral was better than what she had before.

"I'll give you a deep discount—the family rate," is what Chaparral had said. If that was the family rate, she wondered if the non-family rate was better. If you can't screw over family, who can you screw? She grinned at the memory of Lionel's famous one-liners.

Lionel. She glanced at his journal again. She flipped it open to the first page. Inscribed were his name and rank and the division of the military.

US Army (USASC).

What is the USASC?

She flipped the laptop open and did a quick search. Uncle Google told her that the USASC stood for the United States Army Signal Corps.

Signal?

She searched further. And with each sentence she read, her mind raced. He was part of the code breakers of the US Army.

She scanned the property, not looking for anything in specific, but trying to reconcile what this meant.

At that instant, José stepped out of the house. He removed the yellow hard hat, then took off the face mask. The contraption had left a mark on his face. He approached her with a smile.

"Let me get out of my overalls, and I'll give you my assessment," he said.

"I'll get you water," she said.

"That'd be great."

She rose, feeling a bit excited she was triangulating on some break-through with Lionel's mysterious accounting ledger. What exactly caused her to feel excited? She didn't know, but her gut was humming.

By the time she grabbed a bottle from her kitchen and came outside, the others had joined José by his truck.

"So, what do you think?" she asked when she approached them.

"First, the firetrucks came at a very fortuitous time."

Leo put his hand out to Anna, and she high-fived it. If not for Anna, the house and Chicho... she didn't even want to think about it.

"These homes can withstand a lot, but there comes a point of no return. I am happy to say that a good sixty percent of the house is unscathed."

"Seriously?" Cat asked.

"Yup. That doesn't mean they will not need to be updated, remediated, and addressed. There is asbestos in the insulation and the paint. So all that has to be remediated. But that's normal stuff with older homes."

"What about the other forty percent?" Leo asked.

"Needs work. Some areas need a lot more work than others. With the right team, you could have the original house completely done in six months once permits are approved. I can't comment on how long permits could take because that's all a crap shoot."

"But six months of construction is great," Leo said, then turned to her. "Right?"

She grinned. "For sure. That would be amazing. But..."

"How do we find the right team?" José asked. "Yeah, I'll have to make some calls. I think we can find the people. That may take a bit of time, but I'll start right away. In the meantime, I'll write up my estimates of what it will take to get this house back to habitable and safe."

"You're a lifesaver," Anna said. "I'll send you scanned images of the drawings that we mentioned earlier. Will you coordinate with Nicos to get the architectural input?"

"Yes, for sure. There are some issues that I see with the main home as is that will require his input. So we'll package it all up."

Cat was about to cry. For the first time in a long time, these would be tears of joy. Instead of weeping, she hugged the man.

"Thank you!" she said.

"You're welcome, *Mija*. We'll get you all square again."

She welcomed the fatherly hug from José. She hadn't been held with that tenderness since she was in her late teens. Back when her dad was still on her side. Money corrupted so efficiently.

"We have a visitor," Van said.

She released the hold and followed their eyes. Driving at a turtle's pace was Billy in his squad car. Window rolled down, his head slightly tipped enough to see his eyes over the rim of his sunglasses.

The cruiser came to a stop at one moment. Then Billy smiled and drove away.

The Rocas could throw as many of their hired eyes on her they wanted. She didn't mind.

They would not intimidate her. Not this time.

Chapter Fourteen

Leo

Leo tried hard to remember if he had ever really liked Billy. He decided the only reason he had liked Billy was because he had been there. A human coexisting in the same small town, occupying the same space, breathing the same air. What choice did you have?

You went to kindergarten with the same kids, then you graduated from high school with them. They were family. Did you really like that aunt who always smelled like nicotine? No. She was family.

He decided Billy was just an authority-hungry kid who had never grown up from being the undeserving captain of the football team.

Something clicked then. Rafa had been the captain and quarterback for two years before Billy made varsity and took over once Rafa graduated.

So Billy had a connection to Rafa. And with that connection and the perceived power of the badge, he used his authority to serve the needs of his masters.

"Leo, you coming?" Anna asked.

He snapped out of it and realized that José was about to leave. He marched toward José just as he closed his tool chest in the back of the truck.

"Here's what I recommend you do," José said. "Lumber is very hard to find. The lead time is crazy these days. I'll send Anna a text with the type of lumber that I know without a doubt you'll need. They are specifically treated for sea-salt conditions. I would recommend you get that now."

"Yes, absolutely," Cat said.

He hugged Cat and Anna. Shook Van's hand, then when he shook Leo's hand, he pulled him toward the truck's door.

Once they were out of earshot, he spoke. "I have some ideas, but they may get expensive. Should I provide her with the best option for longevity?"

"Absolutely. Only the best."

José winked, then entered his truck and drove away.

"That was awesome," Cat said. "I have hope again."

He grinned. "I think that deserves a hug."

Anna stepped in. "Okay, fine."

He gave her a tepid hug back. "Okay, move on. Next."

"I'm not feeling it," Van said.

Leo stared at Cat, urging her to step up. "Well?"

She rolled her eyes playfully. "Fine."

She stepped into his embrace, and he engulfed her. Could it be possible that someone was built exactly to fit another person's embrace? If so, he was sure Cat was that person for him.

She moved a bit, but he was not ready to release.

"I. Can't. Breathe."

He didn't care. He would hold on to this moment for as long as he could.

Chapter Fifteen

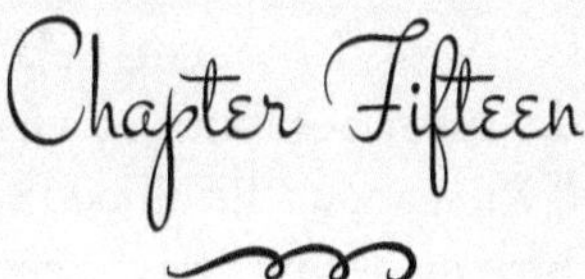

Anna

Anna and Van left the team and rushed across town for their appointment with Lionel's doctor. For a doctor of a small town, Dr. Wang sure couldn't remember anything independently. The power of attorney's letter had set the doctor's mind at ease, but his answers had yet to prove helpful.

His oversized glasses continued to creep down his nose. Each time he leaned toward the monitor, his glasses would slide down, and when he leaned back, he'd push them right back up.

"So, Dr. Wang," Van said, "do your notes refresh your memory?"

"Yes. Um-hm. I recall now. Um. Yeah, odd case. Odd. Um, all peer documentation showed that the protocol we had him on had to work. It's one of those things that—um—you know. It's hard to understand."

Van leaned back. "Can you try to explain it to us? Because we don't understand any of it. Like what could cause something like this? Also, why the treatment was so ineffective?"

Anna liked his approach. Us poor, humble peons know little, oh eminent doctor.

"Sure. Sure. Um. Yeah. So the thing is that we believed a severe ulcer caused this. A bleeding one."

"A bleeding ulcer?" Anna asked.

"Yup, um-hm. Now there are a variety of ways to get an ulcer. Stress, diet, you name it. But in his case," he said as he leaned in, read, fixed his glasses, and returned to them. "Yeah, um-hm, we couldn't really find the source of the blood loss. Twice, I thought we'd found it, but negligible improvements in the end. Frustrating, but also a fascinating case."

"Indeed," Van said. "What about the blood transfusion? What can you tell us about that? Like, how many units was he getting?"

Dr. Wang typed something on his computer and brought up a new screen. From Anna's vantage, she could see that it was lab reports.

"Two units, every two weeks for, let's see...nearly two years."

"Is that typical?"

"Well, no, not really. You see, over time, the bleeding should stop, so over time, you know, no more units needed. Or at least it should drop to one unit and then less often. But not this time."

"In fact, we understand that the two weeks were probably not fast enough," Anna said.

He leaned back and crossed his arms. "No, I don't know about that. I would say that was the right protocol. Yeah. Absolutely appropriate."

His body language screamed with concern. He was worried about a lawsuit.

Anna needed a different approach. "Is it accurate that he'd lose his blood sooner than would've been expected?"

Dr. Wang calmed. "Yeah, um-hm. Two units are a lot. And you know... his insurance." His eyes widened, realizing he'd said what he shouldn't have said. "But anyway. That's all I have for you."

"One more," Van asked. "Can we see his historical HGB levels?"

The doctor brought up a screen, and Van leaned in.

Anna knew Van was up to something. They already had access to those numbers.

"Which are the HGB numbers?" Van asked.

"Um, yeah. This one here that says HGB."

Van studied the screen for a few seconds, then said, "Below 8.0 for almost the duration of his time under treatment."

"Yeah, that's right," the doctor said. "Very low. An adult male should be just above thirteen."

Anna let that sink in. He was at nearly half the normal levels for two years.

"I think we're good," Van said and turned to Anna.

She nodded, and they both rose.

Once they exited the hospital, she tapped his shoulder.

"What were you looking for?" she asked.

"Names of the nurses who took care of him."

He unlocked her door and opened it for her. She slid in. He sprinted to the driver's side and entered the car.

"And?" she asked.

"Only one nurse. Maria Camacho, RN."

"The same nurse each time he was treated?"

"Yup. Maybe it's not that big of a deal, but even for a relatively small hospital, I saw a lot of nurses walking around. So having one nurse do transfusions was a yellow flag for me."

She pulled out her phone. "Let's see if we can find her. What did you think of Dr. Wang?"

He started the car. "I believed him." Van pulled the car out of the parking spot. "Dr. Wang was seriously confused, and to me, he looked like he legitimately couldn't understand why what he tried hadn't worked. It was also clear that he didn't want to be blamed for not doing enough. He even slipped and blamed the insurance for a sec. Probably wouldn't approve more than two-week cycles. You know what I mean?"

But Anna was too busy reading the article she had just found.

"Anna, you okay? You look pale."

She faced him. "Our nurse was in a tragic car accident, days after Lionel Sr. passed away. A suspected drunk driver ran into her while she jogged early in the morning. Per this article, they're searching for the suspect."

Van pulled the car to the curb. "Let me see that," he said and took her phone. His eyes scanned left to right rapidly. He scrolled on until he was done. "I'll find out if they solved the case."

His voice sounded distant.

"Talk to me. What are you thinking?"

"My mind goes to the worst," he said. "Always to the worst."

She didn't want to ask, because she knew what he would say. But she had to hear it. "Which is?"

He turned to her. "She was murdered. If she was murdered, it's because she knew something that was potentially damaging."

Anna shook her head. "Hold on. This is a hypothesis. A radical one at that. We don't know if she was murdered."

"True. But as I mentioned before, I start with the assumption that a crime was committed. And we also agreed that we will look at things through the eyes of everything is connected. If I'm wrong, then we chalk it off as a tragic coincidence. But if I'm right…"

"Then we're all at risk."

Anna and Van knew they could not waste time on this. They needed to speak to Cat and see if she had any insights about Lionel's nurse.

The three huddled inside Cat's trailer. Van stepped through what they had discovered to date. From the medical condition of Lionel Sr., to the treatments and medication that should've worked but didn't.

Cat had her arms crossed for the majority of the time that Van spoke. It was obvious that she was making calculations the entire time.

When Van finished with the findings, she adjusted herself in the seat. "Before we continue, what is your actual role here, Van?"

"He's assisting me," Anna said, knowing full well that this word game would come to an end now.

"What is he assisting with? Are you the same person who Chaparral told me has been given power of attorney by Leo to investigate his dad's medical records?"

"I am," Van said.

"He's a private investigator. And a friend of Leo's," Anna said.

She locked eyes with Van. He didn't blink. "Are you suspecting me?"

"Of what?" he said, unfazed.

"Of anything."

"Too wide a question. I suspect you of a variety of things. But what I'm interested in are criminal matters."

"What he's saying," Anna jumped in, "in his warm and cozy way, is that he does not suspect you of anything illegal or criminal."

"That's a relief." A healthy dose of sarcasm dripped from her words.

"Cat, all Leo is trying to understand is what happened to his father," Anna said. "This is not about laying blame at your feet."

"But you may have some insight that we're missing."

Cat's eyes narrowed.

"You are possibly the only person who can help us understand," Van continued. "So we need your help."

Cat's shoulders loosened slightly. "Okay, shoot."

"Were you with Lionel Sr. each time he went in for his transfusions?" he asked.

"Yes. I took him in and stayed with him. I would leave here and there to get coffee or go to the ladie's room because they were always a couple of hours long. Otherwise, yes, I was there."

"Good," he said. "Now, I want you to think of that room in the hospital. I want you to think of the people who were there. Other patients, doctors, nurses. Just visualize it for me."

"That's easy. There were two nurses there. But every two weeks, when we went in, there were no other patients. And Lionel's nurse was always Maria."

Anna and Van exchanged looks.

"No one else?" he asked. "Always her?"

"Yes. Always her."

"How was she with you guys?" Anna asked.

Cat shifted. "Look, for me, I assume everyone already has it out for me. Even if they don't. So I am hypersensitive. In her case, my impression was that she was doing her job, but she was no friend. She did not make eye contact. Just did the work and nothing more." Cat studied Van and then Anna. "Why the interest in the nurse?"

Van breathed out. "We had planned to ask her questions. Just to be thorough. So the first thing that caught us by surprise is that it was always her for all those years."

"And the second thing?" Cat asked.

Van hesitated, glanced at Anna for confirmation, then spoke. "She died. Just days after Lionel's passing."

Cat covered her mouth. "What? How? What happened to her?"

"A hit-and-run," Van said. "Suspect may still be at large. I have to ask law enforcement friends to give me the latest."

Cat's eyes were downcast.

"What's going through your mind?" Anna asked.

Cat glanced up. "Lionel and I did not have very complimentary things to say about her. She used to miss his vein, which would bruise up his already sensitive skin like a blotch of paint. Like clockwork. Each time. It felt like she was doing it on purpose. So, I filed an official complaint near the end. We were so exhausted... I don't know. When you have such little control over the world, you find things you can control. And I went after the person who I could identify. I feel like crap now."

"That's not why she died, Miss Alonzo," Van said.

"No, I suppose not. It's still very sad."

Anna thought about their theory. No coincidences in any of these things. Cat had confirmed that there was only one nurse and one nurse alone.

And that source was dead under very suspicious conditions. No, this did not feel like a coincidence.

Chapter Sixteen

Catalina

Shortly after Cat had spoken to Anna and Van, Leo had pulled Anna to a work-related conference call. That suited her fine, because she needed to process the news that had been shared with her.

She walked around the property thinking about the nurse and wondered what this implied—if anything. She didn't want to make connections that didn't exist.

She noticed her laptop and Lionel's journal on the picnic table where she'd left them. Just before José finished his inspection, she had made good progress. She couldn't put her finger on it, but in her spirit, she felt like she was close to something important. She needed to get her mind busy and off the passing of the nurse.

She returned to the table, opened up the laptop, and retraced where she'd been when she left the research. She looked at the acronym next to his name.

That was it. Lionel had been an intelligence officer. That had to be significant.

Cat looked at the journal again and flipped to the first page of data. The entry date implied he'd started tracking these over a decade ago. But now that she thought about it, she didn't recall seeing him using the journal in the early years. He'd started to use it near the end.

She looked at the first page and the last page of entries. No evidence of aging. No yellowing, no fading. In fact, it all looked relatively new.

Code breakers.

Was there a hidden message in this book? She went back to page one and looked for anything that might give an indication. What filled the pages were a whole bunch of Yeses, Nos, or blanks in each date's entry. They seemed random, but what if they weren't? What if a pattern repeated on a larger series?

She focused in on a specific pattern and tried to find it again. On the very next page, she saw the exact same pattern. She looked forward to the next five entries and checked on the previous page.

They were a match!

Her heart raced. She opened a blank spreadsheet and typed a 1 for each Yes, a 0 for each No, and a blank for those dates with no entries. She did this for a handful of pages, then looked for the pattern.

It was right there, clear as day. A sequence of 1s, 0s, and blanks followed by a large gap of blanks. That must have been a reset. Or maybe the repeat?

She found the repeating pattern and looked at the sequence. What could it mean? What was obvious now was that Lionel had set this up for Leo or her to find. She was certain of it. He had put the military unit's acronym there as a hint. He wanted them to understand that there was some sort of encryption here.

She put herself in his shoes. If she wanted someone to decrypt a message, what would be the most obvious approach?

Morse. That was the first thing that popped into her head. A quick search gave her the Morse code alphabet. This had to be it. The blank dates must have stood for the break between each letter.

She mapped the sequence to the alphabet and completed the repeating message:

..- -. -. .. . .-. - .... . .-.. . .... -.-

She found a web-based tool, pasted her sequence, and hit Decode.

She nearly cried.

She scanned the property. No one was around. She closed the laptop and hopped to her feet. She ran to Anna's RV, then banged on the door.

Leo opened it. "What's up? Everything okay?"

She smiled. "I cracked the code."

They marched toward the house as she explained what she had figured out. By the time they were in the study, she was ready to reveal the message.

"Well? What did it say?" Leo asked.

"Under the desk," Cat said. "It's hidden somewhere under the desk."

All four leaned down and looked to see if anything obvious stood out.

"I bet it's a hidden door or drawer," Anna said.

"I agree," Leo said. "Let's just push or tug the ornamental pieces and see if anything gives."

"Here!" Cat said.

She could not believe it. A simple button, hiding in plain sight.

"Push it," Anna said.

The excitement in her voice matched what was happening in Cat's heart.

She pressed, and a portion of the wooden wall popped open. It was a hidden drawer as anticipated. She grabbed it and pulled it out. Inside was a metal container, a good six inches deep.

Cat pulled it out and handed it to Leo. They converged around him as he placed it on his father's desk.

Leo slid the latch and lifted the lid. No gold coins. No secret maps to a lost civilization.

Articles. A heavy batch of articles.

"What is that?" Anna asked.

Leo pulled the articles, and underneath them found an accounting journal. He laid the articles to the side and opened the journal. Client accounting books. Detailed analysis of income and expense entries.

Cat touched his hand. "This must be his secret project."

"But what does it mean?" Anna asked.

Leo ran his hands through his hair. "It means that embedded in here is something that my dad thought held answers. He had not been able to land on it. But he thinks I'll be able to. I'll need to go through it all and see what this means."

"What if we got our data analysts to take a first pass at it?" Anna asked. "They'll document them, pull key metadata, make spreadsheets out of the accounting books, and have it ready for you to analyze."

"Tempting. I'm up to my eyeballs at work right now," Leo said. "But he said I should do the work."

"He said you're the only one who may be able to figure it out," Cat said. "Let them pull the data. After that, you can do your thing."

He nodded, then turned to them. "Okay, let's do it. Cat..." He was shaking his head. "I don't even know where to begin. What you did was utter genius."

"Absolutely," Anna said.

"One for the books," Van added.

She smiled ear to ear. "It was sort of cool."

"No, it is epic."

The way he looked at her made her feel alive. She had not lost her zeal for problem-solving. As they stepped out of the house, Cat slid her arm into his.

"I do wonder," he said. "What happened to the one that was meant to be provided to me with the will reading?"

That was a good question. And the answer that came to mind concerned her.

Chapter Seventeen

Leo

They were making dinner plans when Leo's phone rang. He pulled it out and read Chris's name.

He turned away and answered it. "What's up?"

"Urgent meeting. They've summoned all leadership."

The amount of background noise made Chris's voice difficult to hear. "Where?"

"A hangar in Mojave."

He hated the desert. "Fine. When?"

"In three hours."

Leo laughed. "Not gonna happen."

"I'm on my way to you now."

Now he understood the loud background noise.

Leo scanned the surrounding sky. "How far out?"

"Three minutes."

They hung up. "I can't join you guys. Chris is on his way to get me."

"Get you how?" Anna asked.

"Chopper."

"A chopper is coming here? On this property?" Cat asked.

He scanned around. "Right there should be perfect," he said, pointing to an area farther off to the southwest of the house, near a tin storage shed.

"Okay...wow. That's sort of cool. Very *Mission Impossible*," Cat said. "Is everything okay?"

He nodded. "Yeah, should be. It's that new project."

He looked at his truck, and an idea dawned on him.

He turned to Anna. "Download the Tesla app on Cat's phone. You know my credentials." From his wallet, he pulled out the card key for the car and handed it to Cat. "Use the truck for whatever you need. Van or Anna can show you how to charge her up."

"I'm not taking your car."

"Sure you are," he said.

In the distance, he could hear the chopper approaching.

"But I'm not insured."

"My car is insured. But if you're that worried," he said as he went into his text app and typed away a note to an assistant. "There. You're on copy. You'll be added to my insurance. They'll need your driver's license info, probably. Don't be weird about it. Just use the car. You'll need one to get around."

After a long hesitation, she said, "Thanks, Leo."

The sound of the approaching helicopter became overwhelming.

She pulled him close and whispered in his ear, "I'd rather if you were here, instead of your car. Come back soon."

He stared at her as she pulled away. Uncontrollable joy nearly burst out of him. This was quickly turning into the best day of his life.

"Cover your eyes," Van said.

But he didn't bother. All Van did was push his sunglasses tight to his eyes and barely even flinched. These ex-military guys were always so impressive.

The chopper landed smoothly. Chris jumped out of the side door as the chopper's blades wound down.

"I finally get to see this place," Chris said as he jogged not gracefully toward them.

"Professor Anna, good to see you. The tan looks nice on you."

She smirked at him. "You should try it sometime."

They hugged.

He waved toward Van from a distance, then walked up to Cat.

"You must be Cat," he said. "So good to finally meet you."

She gave him a quick hug. "Nice to meet you, too."

Chris looked at her, then turned to Leo. "Man, I wouldn't have left her."

They all froze.

"That was your outside voice, Chris," Anna said.

He looked at her, confused. Then the coin dropped. "Oh, crap. Sorry. I mean...you know."

Cat pushed her hands inside her front pockets. "I appreciate your vote."

Chris appeared to breathe again. "Yeah. No doubt. I only speak the truth."

Leo stepped in. "And before he says anything else, I think it's best we go."

Chris turned to head back to the chopper. Leo was about to follow Chris when he noticed Cat's reddened eyes.

He turned back to her. "What's wrong?"

"I was thinking about Chicho. What he would've given to see one up close like this."

Leo grinned. "Soon enough, we'll give him a ride that he'll never forget."

She nodded.

"You're going to get him back."

She hugged him. This time, she was the one who did not let go.

Chris did not have any insight on what the urgent meeting was about. But it had to be big if all the companies representing the consortium were asked to come within hours of notification. These were not small-time companies that could jump at a moment's notice. And yet, most were already at the private location.

Aram Dersch arrived with two generals. Leo had not met these men before. Their character lines made it no secret that these guys had lost the art of the smile.

"First, I apologize for calling you all like this with little notice," Aram said. "I thank you all for being here on time and respecting our agreed-to ground rules."

Leo scanned the table. Not all were here. He eyed Chris, who seemed to be on the same page. He shrugged. The man missing was a primary contractor to the military for surveillance technology.

"You may have noticed that one of us is missing," Aram said.

Clearly, they would not be coy about whatever had happened.

"Mr. Rustin and his company have been removed from this project."

Audible gasps rose.

"What happened?" one partner asked.

Aram nodded in understanding. "Two things led to this irreversible decision. A couple of months ago, before this project, he began working closely with one of his up-and-coming executives. She had quickly gained his trust. It turns out the trust was more than professional."

Leo turned to Chris. This had suddenly turned interesting, but was somewhat unprofessional to get into people's personal matters.

"It turns out that he had been sharing details of this project with her. As you'll recall, we performed an extensive background search on all parties before we executed the NDAs. There is no wiggle room here. If we haven't done a background search and don't have an executed NDA on file, then they are off-limits. No gray lines."

Leo frowned as he tried to piece it together. There had to be more to this than just pillow talk.

"When we tried to meet with her, she had gone dark."

Leo straightened.

"Apparently, when we contacted Mr. Rustin, she understood the implications and left the city, leaving all her possessions behind. Turns out, she was a Chinese asset who was on a plane returning home. We were able to turn that plane around and arrest her. How much actual information she had and what she shared with her contacts is still unclear. As you can imagine, if her contacts piece this together and release a story through their various contacts in our press... Well, it will be a mess."

Leo breathed out and leaned back in his chair.

"We want to make it very clear to each and everyone of you that nothing can be shared with anyone. One man's actions have placed this entire project at risk. There will come a time that announcements will be made. Until then, we have to keep a tight lid on this."

On the flight back, both Leo and Chris stared outside their windows. Twenty minutes until they reached San José.

"It's a black budget project," Chris said.

Leo snapped out of his thoughts and faced Chris.

"No congressional oversight," Chris added. "This is why they need to keep a tight lid on it. It will come from some unknown fund that was already approved. And once the new Congress is in place, then it can emerge from the black budget and get the full funding."

Leo nodded. "One of the many reasons I've never been willing to work with the government."

"And yet..."

"And yet."

All this under the cover of darkness, cloak and dagger stuff bothered Leo. He was not a conspiracy theorist, but he had his suspicions when it came to the FBI and CIA. You never knew if they were involved.

And once they were involved, you could never get them out of the system. Like a cancer that would take over the host, use it up until the host served no more use. That was dirty business.

What he wouldn't give to just go back to basics again.

Chapter Eighteen

Anna

Anna drove down to San Luis Obispo for a brief ten-minute meeting with Maroutian, the attorney. His office was off the One Highway, near the Madonna Inn.

This was no downtown San Francisco high-riser. Pristine grass and pastel-colored wood sidings complemented this place that felt more like a friend's home than a law office.

She only had to wait a few minutes before Maroutian arrived. He was maybe six feet tall, easily pushing seventy, and rotund. He dragged his feet, nearly wobbling. But the smile on his full cheeks, and his bright eyes, told you a lot more about this man—he was kind and happy.

"So sorry to make you wait," he said. "Follow me in."

Anna did and sat on the cushiony leather chair that he pointed to. On his desk was a brass nameplate on a wood base. Vahe Maroutian Esq.

"Thank you for squeezing me in," she said.

"My pleasure. Time is a precious commodity these days. You see, I'm nearly retired," he said as he slowly lowered himself into his chair. "Problem is, I haven't quite retired. I can never fully leave the practice, so I'm perpetually in between retirement and this." He motioned to his office. "My grandson is in the process of taking over my practice. Whether I'm ready or not, I suspect my wife will force me down that path."

She smiled. Anna had come here with two goals. Information on the will and find an attorney for Cat. "Your grandson practices law also?"

"Yes, he just moved from San Diego."

"What type of law does he practice?"

He reached for a box that lay half open on his desk and pulled a card out. He handed it to Anna. *Zareh Maroutian.*

"He has been focused on family law. But will take on estate law as well."

Thank you, Lord. Thank you for dreams!

"Catalina could use an attorney if he's available," Anna said. "She's in the battle of her life to keep custody of her child."

His bushy eyebrows furrowed. "Ask Miss Alonzo to call the office as soon as she can. I will make sure my grandson takes her case and fights for her." He placed his hands on the rich mahogany desk. "Tell me, how else can I be of service to you?"

Anna made herself comfortable. "How did you know Lionel Moncrieff Sr.?"

"Ah, Monsieur Moncrief. I actually did not know him until the day he called and grilled me for twenty minutes."

This surprised Anna. "How did he find you? A referral?"

"Yelp. That's what he told me. I don't dabble in the social media myself, but since I had something north of three hundred five-star reviews but two one-star reviews, he wanted to know what happened with those one-star review customers. He appreciated the complaints and wanted to know more about them. But I couldn't tell him."

"Confidentiality?"

He nodded. "That's right. He pushed and pushed and pushed. And then eventually he laughed."

"Laughed?" Anna said.

"That's right. He laughed. He told me he needed to find someone who could handle pressure. I told him I'd been married for nearly sixty years and had four daughters, three sons, and a growing army of grandchildren. I could handle any pressure."

Anna leaned back. "Given what you just said about confidentiality, it makes me wonder if you'll answer the next question."

"Might as well try, since you're here."

They both chuckled.

"Did he tell you why he changed his mind about who would be his executor?"

Maroutian seemed to think about it. "Yes. He wanted someone from outside of what he called 'that toxic town.' He wanted no external influence to taint the advice and decision-making. He wanted someone who'd follow the process."

"Did he tell you what made it toxic?"

"No, I'm afraid not."

"Did he say anything about not trusting Roberto Chaparral?"

He studied her, then said, "No, I'm afraid not."

"Is there anything that stood out to you that seemed curious or odd?"

He looked to the ceiling, seeming to search for something to say, then turned his eyes to hers. "He was very concerned about how his son would interpret the will. He wasn't even sure if his son would come to the reading, but he didn't want him to not understand. So I recommended a from-the-heart letter for his son. It seemed this approach helped him have some peace with this hard decision."

"Although I had hoped you'd point me toward the smoking gun, I know Leo will appreciate knowing this bit of information, and it will delight Cat that she may have found her attorney." She shrugged, then rose. "I don't want to burn any more of your time."

He rose with her, but instead of leaving, she tilted her head.

"One last question... Did he, by any chance, tell you anything about the special project that he wanted his son to take over?"

"Ah, yes. Well, very little. You see, Mr. Moncrieff was what I would call a suspicious man. So I recommended he produce copies of whatever it was to assure that Lionel Junior got what he was meant to get. He said he would. But when I asked if he wanted me to be the holder of the material, he said he already had a plan for that."

"Did he tell you who?"

He shrugged. "Once again, I'm afraid he did not."

Anna finished recounting to Van her findings from her meeting with Maroutian. She expected some back-and-forth while she retold the story, but Van had remained silent the whole time, with that silly cigarette dangling from his lips.

And now, even though she was finished, he was still silent, just staring at her. Or maybe through her. She wasn't sure. Through those sunglasses, everything was a guess.

Feeling self-conscious, she took a sip of her ice coffee and waited him out.

But after what felt like minutes, she snapped. "Earth to Van. Any comments? Questions? Feedback?"

His head shifted slightly. He removed the cigarette. "What?"

She leaned forward. "Seriously? I just told you everything I had discussed with the attorney and you were daydreaming?"

He shook his head, then slid off his glasses. "No, I heard everything you said. Sorry. This is just... It's a thing that... Not sure how best to explain it."

"Try by just spitting it out."

He nearly grinned. "Sometimes, when I hear a piece of detail, everything else shuts out. My mind gets hyper-focused on that one thing."

"So you focus intently on a detail," she said passively.

He shook his head. "Not exactly. Imagine you're at a party with twenty, thirty people. And they've brought clowns. Boisterous, crazy, colorful, and loud clowns. Everyone is cheering, and laughing, and some may even be crying because, let's face it, clowns are scary."

"Truth," she said.

"And in the middle of all that chaos, noise, music, and emotional drama is me. I am silent. I am not engaged or interested. All I can think about is the texture of the straw in my hand that's supposed to be plastic, but it feels like uncooked penne pasta."

She looked down at his hand where he was twirling one of those environmentally friendly straws.

"How...?" she started to ask, but didn't know how to phrase it politely.

"Go on. Spit it out," he said, echoing her own words.

She took a deep breath. "Doesn't that negatively affect your work?"

He chuckled. "Just the opposite. That's my superpower. My mind is geared and tuned toward criminal details. The ugly things that people do to each other. The stuff that happens in the shadows. The weaknesses and the flaws that we have. It's not that I'm no longer aware of all the other things that are going on. I still see all the clowns and the people. But I fixate on the thing that matters. The crime."

She grinned. "Those straws do feel criminal at times. But then again..."

"The dolphins, right?"

"Exactly."

They remained silent for a few moments.

"So when I was talking, what did you pick up on?" she asked. "Did you hear a crime?"

He nodded. "Yeah. Someone who knows about the project has purposely kept it away from Leo. This person knows that what we found was something that they did not want Leo to see. And his dad suspected this person could not be trusted. Which is why he made a copy, or copies of it, just in case."

"Right. Right. Good point."

"And we already know one person who Lionel Sr. had clearly identified as not trustworthy."

"Roberto," Anna said.

"Chaparral himself."

"But we have no evidence."

"No, not yet. But once we pick up the scent of blood, we trail it."

Her pulse quickened. "Are you going to surveil him?"

"Yeah. I need to see what he does regularly. But what we don't want is for Chaparral to realize we're onto him."

"To be fair, he may be innocent."

He shrugged. "Maybe. And maybe not. So now that we have our suspicion, we look for the details and the behaviors that are questionable."

"Got it. That's great." She was really enjoying this stuff.

He stared at her. "Don't blow our cover."

She leaned back and crossed her arms. "I'll have you know I have an amazing poker face."

"Clearly."

Her cheeks flushed. *What is that?* Why was she blushing?

"Anyway...what news do you have?"

"Billy, the deputy," he said and got all serious again. "Classic small-town superiority complex. Tried many times to become a cop for the larger cities and he failed all exams. Both physical and psychological."

"So how did he become a deputy in Fortuny?"

"A useful idiot to the powerful in the city. He is the eyes and ears for those in control. He thinks he will become the next sheriff, so if he keeps kissing the right ass cheeks, they will reward him soon enough."

Anna shook her head. "How did you arrive at this synopsis?"

"His past attempts at other departments opened up opportunities for me to contact people I know who are interested in trading favors. The rest of it... My vivid imagination at work filling in the gaps based on everything I've seen of him and stories I've heard."

Anna digested his words as she lifted her cup and stared at him. "Please remember this instruction I'm giving you now. Under no circumstance do I want anyone to hear the cold, surgical analysis you have of me."

He flinched. "You sure? I'm a riot at parties."

"I bet you are." She finished her drink. "Let's get back home."

"Home?" he asked. "That sounds sort of...you know..."

Her cheeks burned up again. She quickly dropped her gaze and stammered, "Y-yeah, home base. Where we get things done." She spun and hurried toward her car.

My goodness, I sound like a motivational poster.

Chapter Nineteen

Catalina

In the span of only four days, Cat's new attorney had prepared a new strategy for the next court hearing. He was organized, confident, and not from the area. All wins.

Roberto had raised some concerns about his experience, but he had not offered her a real alternative. The elder Maroutian had been the bearer of good news when Cat became a new homeowner. Maybe this Maroutian would be the one to reinstate her life with her child by her side.

The courtroom was as it had been in the past session—no family members from the Rocas or the Marcelis. Cat, on the other hand, had both Van and Anna there. Lola was back home, and Leo was once again tied up with the secret project.

The judge had requested various documents to establish how she had been proceeding with establishing a safe, sound, and nurturing home for Chicho.

Judge McAuliffe flipped through the pages of the psych evaluation—a request which had come out of left field. Thankfully, Zareh had predicted it would come, so he had already had her visit a therapist. Highly regarded, experienced, and very expensive. She was hemorrhaging cash, but she'd gladly go broke if it meant getting her son back.

The judge flipped to another page. One temple of his glasses was in his mouth. She wasn't sure if he was chewing it or tasting it. His eyebrows were furled as he focused on the diagnosis.

Zareh turned to her and gave her a friendly smile. He was, at best, in his late twenties, but was already showing some gray streaks in his thick, black, bushy hair. He had impossibly thick eyebrows, the type some women would kill for. His dark brown, nearly black eyes showed care, and the way he spoke showed high intelligence.

"Very good," he finally said. He eyed the Roca family attorney. "This preliminary evaluation gives the court confidence of Miss Catalina Alonzo Marceli's state of mind."

If she didn't know any better, she'd say it annoyed Judge McAuliffe that her team was ready.

"Your Honor, this may have been something that was missed in the transition from her previous attorney to me, but why was this mental health evaluation requested for my client?" Zareh asked.

Great question.

The judge leaned back. "The court received testimony from various citizens that saw Miss Catalina Alonzo Marceli experiencing an emotional breakdown in broad daylight in the middle of downtown Fortuny Bay. Some mentioned that she had been in tears."

Cat's blood turned cold. They had set her up.

"But so far, based on this"—he tapped the paperwork—"I don't see a reason for concern. Therefore, I am stipulating a weekly session until the next hearing. We'll want the standard documentation."

"Yes, Your Honor," Zareh said.

"Now on to gainful employment," the judge said.

Zareh nodded. "Your Honor, we'd like to submit the following for the court to consider—"

"Does she have a job?" the judge asked.

"No, Your Honor. Not exactly."

His glasses' temple went deeper into his mouth as a not-so-friendly grin appeared.

"Not sure what 'not exactly' means in San Diego. Up here, it means no."

Zareh produced a friendly smile. "Your Honor, Miss Alonzo is venturing into an entrepreneurial path. She has the plans, the funding, and the start of a solid business plan to start a bed-and-breakfast in her home."

"A home that is in utter ruins," said the other side's attorney.

The judge glared at him. "You'll get your turn."

He returned his attention to Zareh.

"A home that will be back and running in the next six to nine months," Zareh said.

The judge leaned back. "You say she has funding. If you can show that a bank believes in this venture's ability to generate sustainable income, then produce it."

"Your Honor," the other side chimed in, "the funding is not from a bank nor a real investor. It's from her boyfriend."

Cat nearly leapt out of her seat. But Zareh held her back.

"Your Honor, it is highly irregular for the opposing council to interrupt me while I am producing what you had asked for. If they would be kind enough to wait until I am done, I'll be happy to address their questions and slander at the right time."

A few gasps circled the room.

"Miss Alonzo received an inheritance from the late Lionel Moncrieff Sr. in the form of a home valued at just north of one million dollars and some cash. Finally, the son of Lionel Moncrieff senior, because he wants to see his ancestral home to be restored to what it used to be, has invested in the house's construction. He has gifted that money to the cause. Therefore, Miss Alonzo will not have any debt, whatsoever. This puts her in a financially enviable state. Very few can claim to have that type of financial independence."

The judge took it all in, then wrote a few things down.

"I want to know about the home situation," he finally said. "If she's involved in a relationship, the court must look into the impact that this relationship may have on the welfare of the child."

"Your Honor, Leo Moncrieff Junior is not in a romantic relationship with Miss Catalina. In fact, she is not in any relationship with anyone. The only relationship she is focused on is with her child."

Cat wanted to grab this man and kiss him on his big furry mane of hair. She instead looked over at Anna. She was beaming. They had done well.

"Your Honor," the opposing council said, "there's still the open and very concerning matter of the fire. Per the inspector's report, it is clear that there was negligence involved."

The judge looked over to Zareh.

"Your Honor, with all due respect to the opposing council, the inspector's report is confusing and, at best, incomplete. We ask the court to disregard any insinuations because statements like, and I quote, 'Wood fragments from aging wood sidings observed, which would burn up very quickly.' And this one, 'Observed the presence of lighter fluid,' but he failed to point out that this was beneath the barbecue set which was not the source of fire.

"There are many of these types of details, written and then somehow, he jumps to the summary conclusion that negligence caused the fire. Your Honor, this inspector has not shown causality. He basically says that because the victim has matches in the house, they were irresponsible."

The judge glanced at the opposing council.

"Your Honor, this inspector is respected and is considered one of the best. I am sure he would be delighted to answer any clarifying questions. But he is on leave."

"To be clear, Your Honor," Zareh jumped in, "he has been absent since a couple of days after filing this report, and no one seems to know where he went."

The judge collected his paperwork. "I've heard enough. I want the psychological evaluation by the next time. I also want to see that the ability to earn a living has made significant strides by the next time. We will wait for the fire inspector's return before we complete that piece. Finally, I want a full report from the CPS on the state of mind of the child."

The judge rose, grabbed his things, and walked away. He stopped, went back to his desk, struck the gavel as an afterthought, and left the courtroom.

Cat rose when her attorney did. "Thank you, Mr. Maroutian. That was outstanding."

He leaned in. "You're welcome. Let's button up some of these matters quickly. I want us to be ahead of the curve here. These guys will not give up so easily. And please, do not react to them in the courtroom. I want you to be calm and collected at all times. I don't want them to have any excuses. Particularly since it's evident that they have people watching you. Clear?"

"Abundantly."

He winked at her.

By early evening, Cat had forgotten all the victories earlier in the day, and was back to believing all the worst likely outcomes. She would lose her child.

And even if she won in court, that family would never let her live peacefully.

A knock at her door brought her back to the present moment—splayed out on her couch in the trailer. She dragged herself toward the door.

"It's Anna," she called from the other side.

Cat opened the door, and Anna walked up the steps. "Did you check your email?" Anna asked.

"No, is everything okay?"

Anna grinned. "We got the drawings from the architect." She produced her oversized tablet. "I wanted to see what you thought."

They sat around the table while Anna propped up the tablet. Then she went to the document produced by Nicos Architects LLP.

The very first page, the cover page, nearly had Cat in tears. She plucked the tablet off the stand and brought it close to her face.

"Me too," Anna said and squeezed in.

The rendering of the finished house with the added wings blew her mind away. He had taken Cèlia Moncrieff's drawings and had turned them into a three-dimensional beauty. The foliage around the house, the incorporations of the sandy pathways, and gravel driveway was nothing short of beautiful.

"You're still on the cover page," Anna said. "Open it!"

Cat did. Page after page of drawings. She wanted to make this moment last forever. The interior had an open great room, with wall-to-ceiling bookshelves, a fireplace, and plenty of comfortable seating for dozens of people.

The kitchen was a chef's dream come true. It was organized in a way that the guests could be a part of the experience. The oversized counter gave her an idea where maybe she could teach guests some B&B favorites. Her mind was racing with the possibilities of the things they could do there with the guests.

A mammoth-sized oak table with bench seats on one side and chairs on the other. Complementing that table were five additional round tables for smaller groups of guests who wanted privacy.

She moved on to the bedrooms. How many were there? One after another.

"He's incorporated a dozen guest rooms. Then there are three additional rooms. Your master suite, one for Chicho, and…"

Cat faced her. "And what?"

"Per Lionel's will request, a room for Leo."

Cat couldn't believe that she could have all this. Even a place for Leo. And when not Leo, friends like Lola when he wasn't visiting.

"This is just staggering," Cat said.

"Just realize that if you want to go into full expansion mode, this might cost you most of what you have in the bank."

"The five million Leo deposited?" Cat asked.

"Possibly, because the plan isn't just for the house. There's more to it. A lot of landscaping and grading, so there will be more to do around the entire campus."

"Campus?"

Anna laughed. "Sorry, that's my corporate speak spilling out. But the entire twenty acres will be touched."

"I love everything about this. It's surreal."

Anna shifted in her seat. "Now, for the more challenging part."

"I know, I know. Getting a builder, right?"

Anna nodded. "For one, the builder. But the other part is that we'll have to get the city council to approve this."

Cat's heart dropped. She was right. Those people were stuck in the early 1900a. And worse than that, she was sure a Roca family member held at least one seat.

"Nothing is impossible," Anna said. "But we have to have a plan to build the original structure ASAP. I hope you don't mind, but I've asked the architect to plan a two-phase approach. Build the original structure such that you still have a handful of guest rooms, but if—once—the council approves the expansion, it would be a relatively straightforward path."

"I love that," Cat said.

"By the way, the first batch of the lumber arrives tomorrow. It's the first of four deliveries, but it's happening."

"Awesome," Cat said. It really was all coming together. "I want to meet the architect. I want to add to what he's already done with some ideas I've had. Is that something we could do?"

Anna scooted out. "Absolutely. He had asked to come to the site to see it in person and have a more accurate assessment of the space, the land, and the natural formations around it. The dude's an artist."

Cat got to her feet and handed the tablet to Anna. "So was Leo's mom. A perfect partnership. Speaking of which, has Leo seen it yet?"

Anna shook her head. "Don't think so. He's been in closed-door sessions all day and night. He doesn't even know about the epic courtroom beatdown we had today."

Cat forced a smile. She wanted to celebrate, but tempered herself. With Adela Roca in the picture, bad things could happen in a blink.

That woman did not take losses well. Not at all.

Chapter Twenty

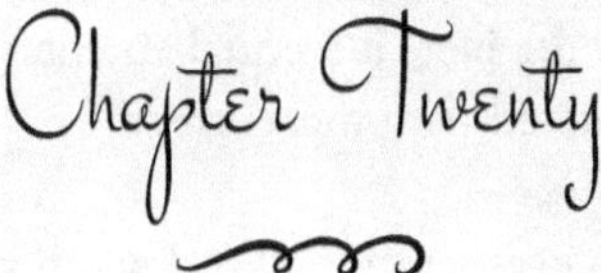

Leo

Leo's driver got him back home at nearly noon. He'd been in meetings with some of the best engineers and designers in the business for...what was it? Thirty-plus hours? That felt about right.

He didn't need much sleep. When he was on, he was on. And when the creative teams were ideating and considering and breaking new boundaries, that's when he felt the most alive.

And yet, he felt like all the amazing breakthroughs would be lost or hidden by the feds. He felt hampered and limited.

Maybe part of the problem was that during the entire time he was there, he kept wondering about Cat's hearing. They had sequestered him with the rest of the team. No connectivity to the outside world. Only one person had permission to disrupt the sessions, and that person would not interrupt even if a fire was threatening the office.

He scrolled through his unread emails. He had over five hundred messages, and that's after his executive assistant had cleared out the solicitations, the things that he did not need to address, and the things that were organized in folders for future follow-up.

"We've arrived, sir," Shmuel said, pulling Leo's attention.

He was a skilled driver, but he was not very good at listening to instructions.

"Shmuel, how long have you been my driver? Three years?"

"Three years, two months, and a handful of days," he said.

"And how many times have I asked you to not call me 'sir'?"

"Although I have not tracked it, I would estimate hundreds of times."

"Right," Leo said. "In fact, it's equal to the number of times you've ever driven me, or interacted with me, correct?"

"Correct, sir."

Leo breathed out in exasperation. "And when will you actually listen to me? I'm your boss. You should probably listen to me, don't you think?"

Shmuel turned to face Leo. His unreasonably brilliant green eyes lit up. "You would not ask me to go against my values and principles. So although I know your goal is to eliminate the hierarchy between us, my training, my life, and my value system make it impossible for me to agree."

"The Israeli Defense Force sure did a number on you."

Shmuel held back a smile. "The moment I forget who you are, and who I am, and why I am here for you, is when I get sloppy."

Leo opened his door, which cause Shmuel to run out to get the door instead.

"Ha, beat you to it," Leo said.

"Yes, sir."

"The only way to fix this impasse," Leo said, "is to fire you."

"An option that is always available to you."

Leo patted him on his shoulder. This man was a driver, yes. But he was also the undercover body guard who had become more and more necessary over the years.

"You're a good man, Shmuel. Your parents should be proud of you."

"Thank you, sir."

Leo grunted, which caused Shmuel to chuckle.

As Leo approached the front door, the car drove toward the underground parking. Shmuel lived on site, but he also had his own apartment. When Leo traveled, Shmuel had full freedom to do what he wanted and where he wanted. He had just come back from a four-week cruise Leo had sent him on right after the sale of Vitruvian.

He was glad Shmuel was back. As much as Leo liked to drive, these long strategy and ideation stages drained him.

He stepped into his house and dropped his bag on the entry bench.

"Hello, Mr. Leo," Leila, his house manager, said.

Well into her fifties, Leila was behind the magic of the house looking showroom ready, the kitchen pantries always well-stocked, all house matters like pool and garden tended to, and bills automagically paid.

"Hello, Leila. How the heck are you?"

"My heck is very well, thank you. But I am worried about you. Have you had breakfast?"

Leo scrunched his eyes. "I think so," he said, but couldn't recall if that was today or the day before.

Leila crossed her arms.

The one time Van met her, he identified her as a typical Middle-Eastern mom. Worried about everything and anything.

"Okay, I will ask a different question. Are you feeling a pain in your tummy? Some people call it being hungry."

He grinned. "I am feeling something like that. A sandwich would be amazing."

"Very well. To your office?"

"No, the kitchen counter would be great."

He washed his face, changed into shorts and a T-shirt, then headed to the kitchen with phone in hand. A turkey club sandwich showed up right in front of him as he sat. A freshly pressed red drink was right next to it. He wasn't sure what it was made of, but he knew it would be amazing.

As he bit into the sandwich, he realized how hungry he really had been.

"Thank you," he said between chews.

"Very welcome," she said.

As he ate and scrolled through his unread emails, he saw one that he had not noticed earlier. From Pete Nicos, the architect.

He opened the email, then double-clicked the attachment. He stopped eating at the sight of the very first image.

"Oh, man," he whispered.

The phone's screen changed just as a call came through. Cat. He quickly pulled an AirPod and popped it into his ear.

"Good morning," he said.

"Morning? It's past noon," she said. "Did you just wake up?"

"Not exactly. My clock is wonky. How are you?"

"I'm great. Did you hear about yesterday's court hearing?"

"Not yet," he said as he rose from the table and walked outside, drink in hand.

She gave him the blow-by-blow as he walked around the pool, repeatedly.

"This attorney has totally come through," he said. "All from that dream of yours."

"No lie. I'm so blessed. And tomorrow I get to see Chicho again."

"Give the little guy a big hug from me."

"Will do."

He could hear the smile in her tone. Her joy brought him joy. This was a simple fact.

"Next topic," she said. "Did you get a chance to see the plans the architect sent yesterday?"

He walked into the sun shelf, the flat area of the pool that was barely four inches deep to keep his feet cool. "I had literally just opened it when you called. What little I saw looked amazing."

"Let's go through them together," she said.

They flipped through the pages, talking about what they loved, what they liked, and what new ideas they could incorporate.

She had just finished talking about the front elevation of the house when she abruptly went silent.

"That's odd," she said.

"What's odd? Something in the drawings?"

"No...I could've sworn..."

"You're killing me here. What's going on?"

"Sorry. We had the first delivery of the lumber yesterday."

"Oh, great."

"Yeah, it is." She hesitated. "Except for the fact that the stash looks smaller."

Leo wasn't sure what to make of it. "Are you sure?"

She chuckled. "Not sure of anything lately. I'll check into it in a bit. I have the manifest. Look, there was something else I wanted to talk about."

"Shoot," he said as he sat on the pool's ledge, feet dangling in the water.

"Next time you're in town, we need to talk about something important."

He threw his feet over and rose. "Coming now."

"What do you mean now? Seriously?"

"I'll be there by late afternoon or early evening. Is that okay?"

She remained silent for a few moments. "That would be amazing. I'll prepare something for us to eat."

After they hung up, he called Shmuel.

"In thirty minutes, we're heading to Fortuny Bay."

"Yes, sir. I'll be ready."

Leo wanted to yell at him, but he was too happy to let that get in his way. He thought he needed rest when he first came home. Now he knew that what he really needed was to see her.

Leo woke up from his nap as the car came to a stop on a gravely road. He sat up and scanned his surroundings. It took him a few seconds before he recalled where he was and why he was in a car.

His door opened. Shmuel offered him a hand.

Leo dragged his body out and stretched as he breathed in the perfectly clean coastal air. No fish guts around here.

"It's beautiful here, sir."

"That it is."

From the look of things, the sun still had a few hours in her before it was time to set. The picnic table was nearly ready for a family-style dinner.

The door to Cat's travel trailer opened, and out she stepped. She wore a long yellow summer dress. Her hair was put up, but a few strands hung over her bare shoulders.

As she set the dishes down, she looked up, then smiled. "Hi there."

He hurried toward her. What he wouldn't give to kiss her, to tell her how he felt. But as he approached her, he knew better. She was not there. Not with Chicho still out with that family.

Instead, he gave her a hug, then kissed one of her cheeks. Her soft skin against his lips sent waves through his body. He hadn't felt this way about another person since the first time she started dating him. And somehow, after they became a couple, he forgot the preciousness of this woman. He'd taken what he'd had with her for granted.

"So glad you were able to drop everything and just come," she said.

"Hey, you never ask for anything. So when you do, I want to make it abundantly clear that my answer will always be yes."

She grinned. "A scrupulous person would take advantage of that."

"A scrupulous person would never get close enough to me."

She held his gaze for a few moments. "Who's your friend?"

He called Shmuel over and introduced her to him. No matter how hard she tried, Shmuel refused to sit at the table and said he would be delighted to eat the food in the car.

Anna and Van emerged from the van. They were chuckling about something. She appeared comfortable and content. Ideas circulated his mind, but he left them there for now.

Van was the first to notice him.

"Boss man," he said and approached Leo, and they hugged. "How was the drive?"

"I slept all the way down. Too tired to trust myself."

"Good thinking," Anna said. "No point in taking chances."

They were catching up when Cat pulled him by his elbow toward the house.

"I'm sorry I dragged you all the way here, when it's probably something that I could've done on the phone," she said. "But I wanted to make sure that we hashed this out in person. Face-to-face."

He blinked. "Sounds dangerous."

"If you agree with me, it won't be."

He chuckled. "Go on. Let's hear it."

She set her jaw and stared directly into his eyes. "I want to partner with you on this."

He tilted his head. "Partner? I told you. This is your home, your project. The money is—"

"Stop. You will listen to me first. Then complain."

He frowned. "Fine."

"Early in my marriage, I realized I was on my own. I had no allies, no one to share with, and no one who could come to my side. Not until I went into complete despair is when the first person stood by my side."

"My dad?" he whispered.

"That's right. Even then, I decided I would do things on my own, my way, without help or favors from others. But when I saw the drawings for the house today...what I saw was your mom's vision, her heart's desire coming to life."

She swallowed and appeared to collect herself.

"Then it hit me. She's *your* mom. This is *your* heritage. Casa Moncrieff carries the names of your family."

"Although all of that is true, this is *your* home."

"Fine, I get that. It is, and I am forever grateful, that this was gifted to me. But when I think of the bed-and-breakfast, when I think of the realization of a dream come true, I know without a doubt that you have to be involved. Not just an opinion here and there, and not just your money. But you need to have an ownership stake.

"This house is a generational blessing. And I know you have more money than most can even imagine, but money is one thing—a generational dream come true... I don't know if one can place a value on that."

He swallowed, holding back the emotions that were rising. He loved his mom more than any bunch of words put together could properly express. On some level, he knew that what Cat was saying was true.

"So what are you saying?" he asked.

"Fifty-fifty partnership. Just using that word is a big deal for me. I think my therapist will call that a personal breakthrough."

"You have a therapist?"

"Required by the court. Separate issue. Anyway, I propose we convert this endeavor and bring it together into a partnership."

He considered her offer.

"Who knows? This may have a positive impact on the court as well," she said. "A formal agreement will show financial backing to see this through without risk that I will be left without money."

"That I can understand."

"And, although I know you don't believe, but I asked God about this. And He said yes. So...you could try to deny me. But you shouldn't deny God."

She didn't know him at all. He could never deny her.

He put out his hand. "Deal."

She grinned ear to ear. Just to witness that smile from this close up would be worth millions upon millions.

She pulled him in for a hug, but she didn't squeeze him. Cat didn't engulf him. She melted into him, and he lost his ability to breathe. He lost sense of time and place. He nestled into this beautiful woman who had found a way to bend him with just her touch.

She pulled away, then wiped at her cheeks.

"Why are you crying?" he asked.

"Because you are in my life again. And with your help, I know I'll get Chicho back again."

He needed to remind himself of who was first. And he knew that if he had been in her shoes, Chicho would first, and everything else, a distant second.

They had finished the lemon garlic shrimp linguini and were waiting for Cat to bring out the epic dessert she had been hinting about. She walked out with a tray of individually sized desserts.

"Crème brûlée?" Van asked.

Leo shook his head. "No, Crema Catalana. My absolute favorite."

"Found your mom's recipe," Cat said.

He just stared at her. She was amazing.

"Thank you," Leo said.

"To Cèlia Casa Moncrieff, and to new beginnings," Cat said as she raised her nearly empty wineglasses.

They all toasted her and drank.

A short while later, Van rose.

"Thank you for including me in this," Van said, "but it's time to head back home."

Leo turned to him. "Where are you staying, anyway? I know they don't have hotels here."

"I'm staying in my home in Santa Barbara," Van said.

"You have a home in Santa Barbara?" Anna asked, the surprise in her voice unmistakable.

"And you drive here every day?" Cat added.

He nodded. "Sure. I'd fly, but I don't have a chopper."

Leo rubbed his tired eyes. "Let's please find a solution that's closer for this poor guy. I'm going to head back to San José in a bit, but I have a driver. You have as many hours to drive as me, and you're on your own."

"I'm fine," Van said, and he sounded like he believed it even though his eyes were bloodshot.

"Well..." Anna said. "You could sleep on the RV's sofa bed. The boss slept on it once."

Van studied Anna for a moment. Leo's eyes darted back and forth between the two.

"You sure?" Van asked.

"Yeah, it's not worth the risk of driving back at this time of the evening."

Van hesitated, then nodded. "If it's good enough for the boss, it'll be fine for me," Van said. "Thank you."

Leo wasn't sure if he was super tired and imagining things, but he was definitely imagining things between those two.

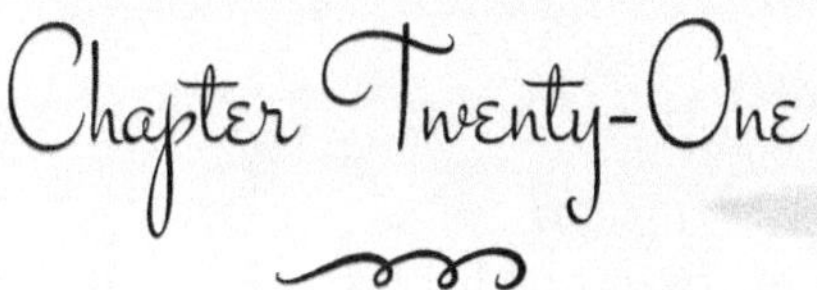

Chapter Twenty-One

Anna

Anna could not fall asleep. She probably should've thought it through more carefully before offering a guy to sleep on her couch. Yes, she had come to know him very well over the past handful of weeks.

And he was nothing but respectful, never weird. Well, he was a bit weird, but not in a creepy type of way.

It's safer this way, she reminded herself. Two single women on an empty lot in a very odd town were the stuff of horror movies.

She flopped to the left. Justifying her actions after the fact was something that she was very good at. But it was still a bit rash of her. She didn't want Van to think there were any ulterior motives. And she certainly didn't want Leo to think that something was brewing here.

He's going to ask.

She was sure of it. The way he grinned, she was sure he'd want to know more.

And then there was Cat. She didn't want Cat to think that she was a one-night stand type of person. Because she was not.

I did the decent thing.

That's exactly what it was—the decent and Christian thing to do.

Then why could she not fall asleep? Suddenly, a loud, grinding noise rose in the RV.

She sat up.

And there it was. The dude was a snorer.

Great. Just great!

By the time Anna emerged from her room, Van was already up and writing notes. He was old-school. Pencil on little notepads.

"Morning," he said while he wrote away.

"Hey," she said. "Slept well?"

"Like a baby."

Glad you *did.* "Good to hear."

"Did my snoring wake you?" He stopped writing and glanced at her.

"No, not exactly."

He grinned. "What does that mean?"

She walked over and sat across from him. "When you started your nostril syncopation orchestra, I was still awake. So, no, you did not wake me."

He laughed. A legitimate belly laugh she had never heard from him.

"A nostril orchestra?"

"Syncopation orchestra. Various instruments all over the place."

He grinned, wiped at what must've been a tear. "You are actually quite funny."

She shrugged. "I have my moments."

Anna made tea for both of them and handed one to him as he looked through the small storage container that had Lionel Sr.'s documents.

"They brought this back from the office?" Van asked.

"Yes. Thanks to you, I trust no one. So I had an analyst from work digitalize it then bring back the originals."

"You mean scan it?"

She grinned, then took another sip. "Much more than that. Searchable scan, yes. But then the information is extracted into a very sophisticated database. Think of a very intelligent robot that scans through the documents and finds connections."

"This the artificial intelligence business I keep reading about? So our working theory of everything is connected on a digital platform."

"Exactly. Any secret hiding in those documents will be brought under light, and they will be exposed." She stared at the tattoo of the ornate cross on his arm. "What's the story behind the tattoo?"

He looked at it almost as if studying it for the first time. He ran his index finger over the design. "It's called *khachkar.* It's the Armenian cross stone. A promise I made to my grandmother. She died during shelling by the Azerbaijan army. I promised I'd try to make sense out of her insensible death. That I'd figure out God's plan."

She waited him out for a couple of seconds. "Did you? Figure out God's plan?"

He shook his head. "No...but I am a patient man."

He grabbed her cup and his and took it to the sink. He washed the cups slowly, then turned to her.

"Was thinking about what you said about placing secrets under the light. What happens when a wild animal that has prowled in the dark is suddenly exposed by light?" he asked.

She thought about it. "Well, at first they freeze."

"Correct," he said. "The classic deer-in-the-headlight saying. But then, the wild animal does what it must. It attacks."

She considered his analogy. "Survival instinct."

"Nothing more dangerous than man's primal need to survive."

She rose. "What are you suggesting?"

"Whatever we discover, we need to be ready that initially there will be shock and a pause. But then..."

"Counterattack."

"At all costs."

Chapter Twenty-Two

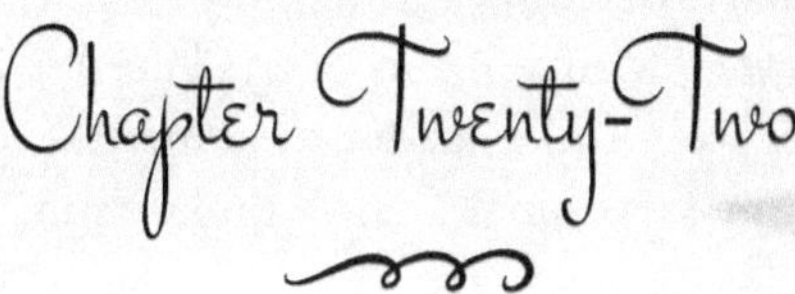

Catalina

Cat parked the beast of a truck in the rear parking lot of Child Protective Services. She felt silly driving this type of car, but it was a safe and comfortable drive. Right now, safety was top of mind.

She grabbed her purse and rushed into the building. She was early, but she did not want to miss one minute with him in the event Chicho was already there.

Unfortunately, he arrived fifteen minutes late. When the door opened, he ran into her arms. She lifted him up and spun him around.

"How are you, Mama?" he asked while she was still squeezing him tightly, with her eyes shut.

"With you in my arms, I am perfect," she said.

Cat lowered him and looked up. Behind him, still at the entrance of the door, was Maggie, who was closing it behind her.

On the other side of the door was Elizabeta Marceli. Her long, straight black hair reached her chest. Her perfect cheekbones glistened even under the harsh lights of fluorescent bulbs.

No smile. No emotion other than contempt. Like she was looking at the excrement of a half-breed mutt.

When Maggie closed the door, the air returned to Cat's lungs. She walked Chicho by the hand to the couch and sat down. That's when she noticed his clothes.

"What's this?" she asked him while tapping his shirt.

"It's my new clothes, Mama. Abuelita says I need to look the part."

She clenched her jaw. "And what does that mean?"

He shrugged. "She says things I don't understand. But she's nice, so I smile."

"She's nice to you?"

"Yeah. Everyone is nice."

She studied the clothes he had on. Polo shirt, shorts that were made for the country club, and high-quality leather loafers. Gone were his Batman T-shirts, bargain-bin shorts, and hand-me-down sneakers.

"Well, you look very handsome," she said.

"Thanks. When will you come and stay with us?"

Cat flinched. She glanced at Maggie, who was emotionless. "I don't think that's the plan, sweetie. I'm fixing our house right now."

"The one that burnt down?"

"Yes. So that we can be together again. Me and you."

He seemed to chew on her words. "But I'm afraid of that house. We might die in it."

Her eyes widened, but she quickly collected herself. What was that family feeding him? "I can understand why you'd worry, but I want you to know that we will be super safe. You know why? We're making it so strong that even Batman will want to live there."

He smiled. "Really?"

"Really. You'll love it once you see it."

He frowned. "Okay, Mama."

They had been chatting and drawing for a few minutes when he stopped and went back to the couch.

"Are you okay?"

He crossed his arms. "I don't remember my dad."

She joined him. "Yes, you were very young when he passed away."

He fidgeted with his clothes. "But I don't have pictures of him either. Or videos."

She could feel Maggie's eyes on her. "You're right. When we first moved into Lionel's house, we never opened our boxes and put out picture frames or albums."

He looked at her. "Why?"

"We didn't know how long we'd be there. We didn't have a place of our own. But we do now. This time, when we move into the fixed-up house, we will decorate your new room with any picture you want."

He smiled. "Good. I want pictures of my dad like I have in my other new room. I miss him."

Her face flushed. "Of course. That's a good idea."

He hopped off the couch and went back to his drawing. He continued to draw a garden. She joined him.

"That's beautiful," she said.

His skills at art had improved in the two weeks since they had taken him away.

"Thanks. Miss Lake is teaching me how to draw."

Her heart sank. "Miss Lake is an art teacher?"

"Yeah. Abuelita has her come over to teach me. She comes a lot. But I don't mind. I like her. Abuelita says I shouldn't waste time by doing nothing. Another teacher will come to teach me new things. Abuelita said I don't have to go to school, but she will bring school to the house."

Homeschooled? Cat wasn't sure if she should be mad or grateful. On one hand, when it came to his art, this is what Cat had wanted to do for her son. Now, Adela or Elizabeta had done it. And they had made a decision on his schooling without involving her.

The Rocas were doing everything they could to align Chicho with them and, at the same time, keep her out of the decision-making process.

This was not good. She had to speed up the custody hearing.

She had just hopped into her car when her phone rang. Her attorney.

"Hi, Zareh. You read my mind," she said. "I just saw Chicho and have some concerns."

"Sure. You go first," he said.

"I want to accelerate the custody decision."

"I don't think that's wise. Too many open matters," he said.

"How about temporary shared custody?" She pulled the car out of the lot. "They're brainwashing him."

"Explain?" he asked. His voice took on a grave tone.

"Maybe I'm exaggerating by saying brainwash, but he's being altered. His clothes are all country-club style. He's talking about me moving in with the Rocas. He even started asking about his father and saying how he missed him. He doesn't have any independent memories of that man. They're putting pictures of his father in his room and changing the narrative."

He breathed out. "I hate to be insensitive, but as said in politics, elections have consequences. They have the upper hand and can do what they think is proper. From the foods he eats, to the clothes he wears, and to the memories he'll recall. You, in effect, were doing the same when he was with you."

"I never bad-mouthed that family," she said as she took the turn onto the freeway.

"I'm not suggesting that you did. But by excluding them, it was, in effect, indirectly messaging to Francisco that they were not part of the team."

She blinked heavily. "So, what can we do?"

"We can take a shot at a different visitation protocol. He could stay with you for a couple of days out of the week, and so on. Anything more aggressive could cause the court to want more evidence."

"Okay, something is better than nothing."

"I'll start working on that. Now, as to the reason I called. I assume you have not checked social media?"

She laughed. "No, I am not a social-media type of person."

"Well, you are now. You and Leo are showing up everywhere. A British rag has an entire story about you, about him, about you and him."

The buzzing all over her body escalated with each passing word.

"It's not a good look. I am not a PR person, but I assume Mr. Moncrieff has an army. You'll want to get them to help manage the narrative. This might have a negative impact on the court."

"Understood," she said, her voice barely audible.

"Sure. And please be careful. I do not think it's a coincidence that this is happening now. Just like I don't think it's a coincidence that people in town reported to the court that you were crying in the streets."

She shook her head. "No. Nothing is ever a coincidence with the Rocas."

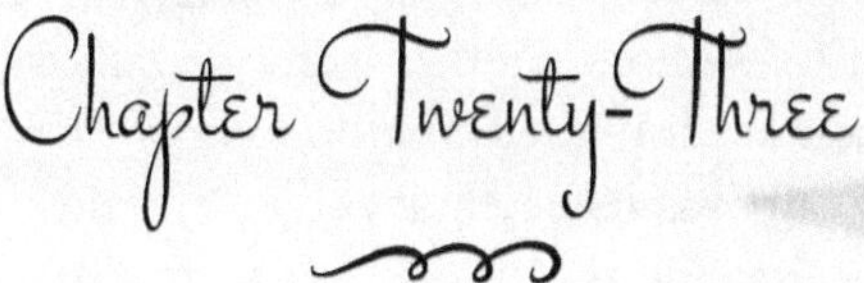

Chapter Twenty-Three

Leo

When Leo had entered his 8:00 a.m. meeting, there were no unread messages left on his phone. When he reemerged from the conference room at half past one, he had hundreds of messages. Texts, emails, and all other types of notifications.

What the—?

"Leo," Francine, his assistant, said, "Jeff from public relations is ready to jump on the news reports. Do you want me to cancel your 2:00 p.m.?"

"What news reports?" he asked as he tried to catch a glimpse of the Tweets and Instagram posts. They rushed down the hallway toward his office.

"You don't know?" she asked, to which he responded with a look that made it clear that she asked the wrong question. "Sorry. A few rags are running a story about you and your new love affair."

"What love affair?"

They reached his office.

She closed the door behind her, then rushed over to his computer. "Jeff sent you an email with a compilation of the major headlines and summary points and recommended actions."

He sat behind the desk and opened the email. "Can you get me a bottle of water and a double espresso, please?"

"Sure, but just so you know, your salad is sitting on your conference table." She pointed toward the table that overlooked the city.

He glanced at it. Without another word, he pulled his laptop, walked over to the table, and made himself comfortable.

"Let's see what all this excitement is about," he said.

He opened the first link as he forked a large dose of greens and shoveled it into his mouth.

"'Billionaire Leo Moncrieff in a steamy new relationship,'" he read.

The picture gave him pause. It was from the night before. He and Cat caught in an embrace. Admittedly, the paparazzi had captured a good moment—grainy, but good. It looked like there was more behind that hug. Maybe because there was.

"So far, I'm not seeing anything concerning," he said.

"Go to the third one," the assistant said.

He eyed her.

"Trust me. The third one."

He clicked on it and immediately knew why this one was problematic.

The headline read, 'Gold digger moves on to the next conquest.'

"Well, crap."

The next line said, 'Femme fatale lover who is still under investigation for the death of husband has her hooks into ex-lover and now tech billionaire Leo Moncrieff.'

He scanned the article. This was bad. They made insinuations accusing her of plotting her husband's death.

He read a line that stopped him in his tracks. "Listen to this crap. 'With her child nowhere in sight, she created a perfect setting for a romantic night with her past lover.'"

He looked at his assistant in shock. "Child Protective Services took the child away. That's why the kid's not there."

She flinched. "Why? What did she do that they would take away her kid?"

Great, just great.

"Nothing, they're out to get her. Call in Jeff."

"You got it. By the way, check out the seventh one as well."

He pushed his salad away. "Go. Get him."

As she closed the door, he opened that article. A picture of him emerging from the car. The way they had changed the colors and image saturation, he looked like a junky.

'Returning from a night of partying and who knows what else, billionaire Leo Moncrieff goes to his lover's beach house.'

"This is just stupid," he said just as Jeff walked in. "Sit. Can we just kill this?"

Jeff shook his head. "It's already doing the cycles internationally. But really, it's a nothing-burger. It'll die on its own. They've had even worse pictures of you from the past."

"Thanks for the reminder. But I don't want this to mess her up. What can we do?"

But before they could exchange ideas, his phone rang. It was Cat.

"That's her now," he told Jeff.

He answered it and put it on speakerphone.

"Hey, did you see the articles?" she asked.

"Yeah, I did. We're gonna see what we can do to derail it."

"I'm so sorry," she said.

"Why are you sorry? This isn't your fault." He eyed Jeff, who looked just as confused as Leo.

"Leo, I don't believe this is about you. It's the Rocas. They are coming after me by going after you. It's an indirect way of discrediting me as a mom."

Leo sat back in his chair. He connected the dots. Was she right?

"It would be great if there's anything your side can do to spin this favorably. Otherwise, I have to lie low so that the court doesn't throw this in my face."

"Give me a sec," he said, then muted the phone. "Jeff, make that your prime directive. How to best spin this. I don't care what they say about me."

Jeff grimaced.

"What's on your mind?" Leo asked.

"The special project. We don't want you to look too bad in this either. Otherwise..."

Crap. He was right. "Fair enough. Some damage control is appropriate. But I want her to be cleared. Even if it's the threat of legal action. Get the team to think out of the box."

"You got it," he said and left the office.

"Okay, I'm back," he said. "I asked my team to come up with something to help. That family is a piece of work. You sure know how to pick them."

"If you only really knew," she said.

"What does that mean?"

"Nothing. It doesn't matter. It's been a rough day." She paused. "Anna and Van just pulled up. They need to know what's going on. Let me pull them into this call."

Ten minutes later, via the phone's video conferencing application, they were done debating if it really was the Rocas or classic paparazzi and rag behavior.

Something distracted Cat.

"What's wrong?" Leo asked.

"Are you kidding me?" Cat said. "Half my lumber is gone."

"Do you mean someone's stealing it?" Leo asked.

"Most likely," Van said.

Cat's eyes filled with rage.

"Give me a sec," Van said as he walked around the remaining lumber.

He knelt, studying the dirt, then followed what might have been tire tracks toward the street.

He jogged back. "Tire tracks came in—most likely Goodyear Wranglers. Reversed out with a heavy load in them. I suspect they couldn't fit more. Probably planning for a second and third round."

"I can't believe they'd do this," Cat said. "While I was at CPS and you guys were investigating."

"Not to get paranoid, but are we thinking it's the Rocas?" Anna asked.

"No doubt," Cat said.

"I agree," Van said. "I recommend a police report and an insurance claim."

"Hold on," Cat said. "Let's think this through. If I file a police report, what will that say to the court?"

Silence.

"Well, crap," Anna said. "I see your point."

"If I chase this, it'll backfire. They're trying to show that this is an unsafe place for Chicho. That I have no control over my environment. A police report will play right into their hands."

More silence.

"She's right," Van said.

"Agreed," Anna added.

"I've heard enough," Leo said. "Anna and Van, this is our new game plan. I want temporary perimeter fencing around the property. I want it tall, ten feet with privacy meshing. The gate should be solid and mechanical so that you guys can easily come in and out.

"We may not be able to get it along the entire twenty acres, but in the interim, let's get fencing at least in the front and the sides that reach the hill formations so that it's not easy access for anyone. More material is bound to be delivered. We don't want this stuff to just walk away. Also, I want security cameras everywhere. We need to keep you all safe."

"What about guards?" Van asked.

"Sure, whatever you think is appropriate."

"I can pull some favor and have a team here in twenty-four to forty-eight hours. In the meantime, I'll stay overnight until we get the team set up."

"Thank you, Van. I owe you one," Leo said. "Cat and Anna, we'll get you safe."

Cat's eyes were downcast. Her demeanor was subdued.

"Hey, speak to me," Leo said.

"To protect ourselves, we have to create our own prison and stay inside of it. Something feels very upside down about this."

Chapter Twenty-Four

Anna

When Cat cut the call with Leo, Anna instinctively placed an arm around her shoulder and pulled her in.

"You gonna be okay?" Anna asked.

Cat looked up. "Yeah, I will be. So much going on. With Chicho, the news stories, and now the lumber theft. It's relentless. I can't even seem to gain traction with the house. Even José is hitting brick walls. I wish he'd just say yes and do it."

"You want me to ask?"

Cat's eyes widened. "You think he would?"

"Asking is free. He seemed to be excited about the project. Yeah, the logistics may be tough for him to pull, but...who knows."

"Yes, please. Let's try. That would be amazing," Cat said.

"Also, I know he enjoys working with the architect. So that may be something that would entice him as well. The budget may take a hit with the additional travel and boarding expenses for him."

Cat frowned. "Hadn't thought about that."

"We'll make your business partner cover those costs."

Cat grinned. "I'll leave that to you. I like how you have simple, straight-forward ideas for problems. If only we could find an easy solution to stop them from spreading more lies."

Anna shrugged. "I have a solution for that, too. You may not love it, but I have a recommendation."

Cat studied her. "I'm listening."

"First, you two have to figure out what you are to each other. Then, whatever that is, embrace it, don't hide it, and let the press say what they want."

"But what if all we are and all we'll be are good friends?"

Anna nodded. "Then I recommend you learn how to hug like good friends hug."

"What does that mean?" Cat's cheeks picked up a few shades of pink.

"It's not an accusation. It's an observation. When you two hug, you guys look like the world disappears. It's a beautiful thing to have that type of connection. But to the outside world... Well...you get the point."

Cat blinked. "I do. But...how can I even think about anything else when those people have my kid?"

"You're right. That is what matters. Having said that, we all need help. We need friends. We need partners. And sometimes we need something more...to remind us of what makes us human."

After Anna tossed the trash bag in the trash bin, she saw Van position his car such that it partially blocked a portion of the driveway. He turned off the car, then strolled to the trunk and pulled out a sleeping bag.

She slowed her pace and considered her options. She had a sofa bed in her RV. He had just used it a few days ago. So she could invite him again. But then again, she didn't want him to get the wrong idea.

He yanked the rear door open and rolled out the sleeping bag.

She thought about it again, but decided against it. She didn't want to open a door that would be hard to close later.

She thought of the advice she'd given Cat earlier. If she didn't want to create confusion, then she needed to stop creating openings that would lead to misunderstanding.

She glanced at him once again before entering her RV. He was no longer outside. He had made himself comfortable.

He's used to this.

After all, he was a private investigator. He probably had to do this type of stuff all the time. Which is precisely why he had a sleeping bag in his car.

She felt good about the decision. This was the right approach.

And if she was being honest with herself, she was getting too used to having him around. Having him in the RV at nights just seemed like an invitation that she was not ready to hand out.

Chapter Twenty-Five

Catalina

Two days later, Cat anxiously awaited the visit with the architect, Pete, and José. After a brief deliberation, José had said yes to the work.

In the initial phases, his foreman would lead the work until another project wrapped up. At which point, José would stay locally three days out of the week and manage remotely the rest of the time. The financial impact was minimal.

Finally, momentum.

Despite the unfortunate press that had been hounding her and Leo, at least when it came to the house, things were finally falling into place. With the start of the construction, she'd have an excellent case for partial custody. Her attorney was also hopeful, which meant she wasn't just living on hopes and dreams. So much so that he had requested a hearing on that very topic in one week.

Chicho will come home soon.

She was also glad to see that the security plan was coming together. Van was currently with the fence installers. They had finished digging trenches for the fence footing. The more she learned about construction and land development, the more she found that she really enjoyed the way something old could become new. How, from nothing, something beautiful came.

She recalled what Anna had said shortly after the fire. *From these ashes, you will rebuild something beautiful.*

Thanks to this team, these partners of hers, that was, in fact, what was about to happen. All she needed was her beautiful boy by her side. She wanted him to witness all this.

A heavily tinted car pulled into the dirt driveway.

"Leo?" she said.

She was not expecting him to join them. She picked up her pace.

The driver opened the door, and out came Leo.

He wore perfectly fitted jeans and a T-shirt—no logos, no marks. It was tight at the shoulders, stretching the cloth over his chest. The veins visible in his arms told her he was exercising again. Unlike when he had been in Fortuny Bay during those brief days.

He marched with the phone pressed to his ear, but as he approached her, he hung up then looked at her. His smile was like sunlight.

"Surprised?" he asked as he reached her.

"Very," she said. "Is it safe to hug?"

"Just don't drool all over me, and we should be safe," he said.

She glared at him, then gave him a quick embrace. She had taken Anna's advice to heart. She needed to check herself. But boy, did he smell nice.

"So glad you're here."

"Me too. Wasn't sure if I could pull it off, but I've got a small window before I have to head back again. Wanted to see what the architect had to say and how soon José planned to start."

"Hey, Leo," Van said.

Anna jumped out of her RV.

"They'll let anyone in here!" Anna said.

They all huddled.

"How goes the security?" Leo asked.

"Good. Forty-eight hours and we'll have full perimeter fencing. We already have on-site security, but two more days we'll have twenty-four-hour guard service. Three people, three shifts."

"Excellent. How's your back?" Leo asked.

Both Cat and Anna turned to Van.

"You hurt your back?" Cat asked.

He shook his head. "I'm fine."

"Sleeping in cars is not as romantic as it sounds, is it?" Leo said.

"Just a couple of more days and the service will be in place. Not a big deal."

Two cars pulled into the property. José's truck followed by a convertible. Someone else was in José's truck. But Cat focused on the two inside the convertible, which must've been the architect.

The architect, Pete Nicos, stepped out. He was tall. Very tall. He studied the house, then smiled. He must've approved. He said something to his passenger, and she nodded in agreement.

Her light-streaked hair lifted with the ocean breeze. She grabbed a baseball cap, slid it on backward, then yanked another bag. From it, she pulled out a camera.

They walked toward the huddle.

"Sorry for running late," José said. "Long road. This is Oscar, the foreman, and my right-hand man who will handle the day-to-day. I will join the party soon enough, but you can trust him completely. And these are Pete and Sophie."

They all shook hands, but Sophie hugged both Leo and Anna. She must've known them.

"If you don't mind," Sophie said, "I'm going to scout the area."

Her smile was both beautiful and elegant. She looked like Jessica Alba meets...well...Jessica Alba. Without another word, Sophie marched off.

"Miss Alonzo—" Pete said.

"Cat, please," she corrected.

"Cat, I love this house," Pete said. "It's even better than what I had envisioned from the pictures. Sophie will take pictures of everything. Including the terrain all around it. I'm a firm believer that the best architecture is not the one where the architect can boast about their design genius. Architecture, for me, should be invisible. A home should blend in the natural environment. With this house, we want to celebrate its history and its prominence."

He spun toward the city view. "This beauty perches above Fortuny Bay," Pete continued. "It has a royal feel to it. I feel this house should be an inviting beacon for visitors. That when they come here, they feel like they have walked into a place that they never want to leave. Not willingly, at least."

He searched Cat's eyes. "Thoughts?"

Cat swallowed back tears. "When can you start?"

They spent the better part of four hours going over the initial proposal. She was absolutely loving this man's energy and enthusiasm. They were redlining, writing notes, coming up with new ideas, and overall having a blast at taking the existing beauty of the home and expanding it without making it look out of place or gaudy.

The entire team put on hard hats and entered the house, where Pete pointed out what he wanted to preserve and what he wanted to radically change.

"I was curious," Pete said when they were walking back downstairs. "Do you know if this house is considered historic?"

"Doubt it," Leo said.

"What about the architect? Any clue who designed it?"

"Sorry," Leo said. "I think my great grandparents designed and built it, but that was the story that was handed down."

"The Casa family, correct?" Pete asked.

"That's right."

Pete made a note of it on his pad. "I'll see if there's anything in the literature on this house."

"Why would that matter?" Cat asked.

"Well, if it is historic, then we would want to include the right organizations. Preservation takes on a different meaning for historic homes."

"Interesting," Leo said, but then they moved on to the living room area.

"Some of these rooms will need to be gutted," José said. "The damage is considerable. But I'm sticking with my initial estimate that sixty-percent of the house is salvageable."

"Having said that," Pete said, "all the walls will open up. The house is old. It needs its innards to be upgraded to code and made to last another one hundred years."

"I like the sound of that," Leo said.

Once they were done touring the house, they all stepped outside.

"What about permits?" Anna asked.

"Oscar will pull licenses immediately for some of these activities. The core work will be fine. After the architecture is completed and the engineering is signed off, then we have to pull permits to extend the house's wings."

"But all the demo, cleanup, prep can be done without permits?" Cat asked.

"Not exactly," José said. "There's an entire process when it comes to fire cleanup and inspection of the house for potential lead in the paint and asbestos. So we'll need permits for that which are already in progress. A specific team comes out for that part, and we'll be told how to handle any and all contaminated materials."

She frowned.

"Don't worry. This is not new science. We've done it many times before. We should have those first permits in our hands by end of day. If all goes well, we'll start in a couple of days," José said with a grin. "I know you want to move fast. We will get to that finish line for you and your son."

She shrugged. "Can't help myself. I have a one-track mind."

They all exited the house, went by the picnic bench, and grabbed water bottles.

"What ideas do you have for the path to the beach?" Leo asked.

Pete was about to show them something on his very large tablet when Leo's phone rang. He stepped away to answer it.

He said a few words, then came back looking agitated.

"Are you okay?" Cat asked.

"Nothing that can't be dealt with."

Anna gave him a look, and he shook it off.

"I'll need to take a call in your RV in a few minutes," he told Anna.

Cat knew that look.

Something was wrong. She hoped it had nothing to do with her.

Chapter Twenty-Six

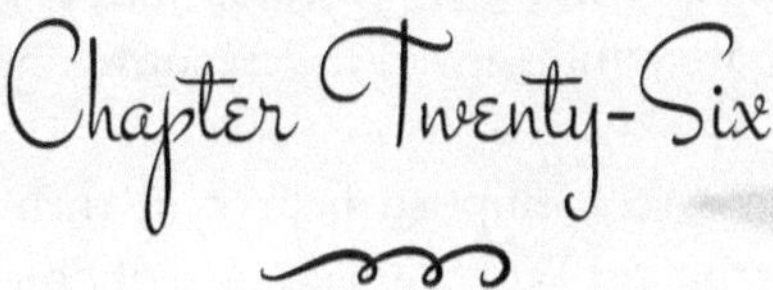

Leo

Leo grabbed his laptop from the car, then went into Anna's RV. He plopped the computer on the desk, snapped open a bottle of water, and connected to the secured video conference bridge.

He liked Aram Dersch. But he didn't like his cryptic text messages. Mainly because they could mean anything. The one he had just received being exhibit one.

Call. Hot.

Each sentence only one word long. Each word and their order produced multiple interpretations.

But with Aram, there were really two reasons he'd text. Good news or bad news. Given the amount of work he and his team had been burning on this secret project, he wanted to hear good news. No, he wanted to hear epic news. Like some major player had joined the team, or the government would have zero oversight. But deep down, he knew this call would end up annoying him.

Aram's face came into focus.

"Hey, Aram. What's up?" Leo asked.

"Sorry about the fire drill," he said.

That settled it. Not good news.

"What happened now?"

"Well..." He broke eye-contact for a moment, then fixed his eyes back on the camera. "It's not what happened, but what might happen."

"I'm tired. Can we get to it? What are we talking about?"

"You and the press. Once this project is announced, it will be global news. The last thing we want is any of the executives involved to be part of a scandal."

Leo grabbed his water, emptied half of it, then set it aside. "What scandal are you referring to? What am I accused of now?"

"Maybe scandal is too big a word."

"Look at that. A real-time reduction in sentence. What is it you're worried about?" He registered the pain in his hands. They were rolled up into fists, so tight that his nails had dug into his palms.

"Your association with a woman who is accused of killing her wealthy husband is taking a life of its own," Aram said. "The articles and direction of the news cycle is that you are a playboy billionaire—"

"Like Bruce Wayne," Leo interjected.

Aram's jaw clenched. He didn't look like he was loving Leo's humor. "Leo. You and I go back. You know I love you."

"I do," Leo said.

Aram loved the money he had made by betting on a horse that kept winning.

"But you need to realize this is the next level. You are part of an elite group of executives. You have a seat. A well-deserved seat. But with that seat comes the responsibility to come across as stable, reliable, and brilliant. You can't be seen in Vegas nightclubs getting hammered. You can't be associated with women who draw the wrong type of attention to you."

"Stop," Leo said. "That woman was my girlfriend in high school. She was the one I promised to marry someday. She was the one who took care of my dad when he was dying. So *that woman* is not just another woman."

Aram blinked, then nodded. "Was not aware of that."

The silence stretched out.

"Here's what I recommend," Aram said. "Keep it private. No outdoor events. No opportunities for these jackals to get pictures at the wrong microsecond. Keep it all under the radar."

"Working on that already."

"Good. Look, I'm sorry. I can see this is not a straightforward situation that you're in. I want you to succeed. So I will do everything I can to help you succeed. Including getting my nose into business that's not mine. But you know our world better than most. Sometimes we make sacrifices. Sometimes we get sacrificed."

Leo gathered himself and walked outside to join the team. They were all smiles and laughter.

Glad someone's having a good day.

That wasn't fair. Up to that call, they were all riding the wave of excitement. He would anchor himself in that conversation, not the silliness of rags and paparazzi and crazy family drama.

If this were indeed the doing of the Roca family, then they were taking this to a new low. He wondered if a face-to-face with Adela was what was really needed. They needed to reach some form of a mutual understanding.

Maybe he could get her to see that what she was doing would not help Chicho. But instead, imprint the poor kid with the type of damage that could last a lifetime.

"All good?" Anna asked.

"All will be good."

She nodded, but did not break eye contact with him. She knew something was up. He'd share with her later. Not in front of Cat. She had plenty on her mind already.

Cat strolled up to him and just smiled. "Thank you."

"For what?"

"What the architect and José have shown us... The potential. This is really happening. We are going to make your mom's and your grandmother's dreams real."

He grinned. "Yeah, that is pretty cool."

She hugged him, her face on his chest.

He hesitated, recalling Aram's words. But then the reality landed. Leo wanted her to hug him. He wanted to hold her. He wanted to be with her. He let go and planted a warm kiss on the top of her head.

For a second, he thought he saw movement from the hillside. He scanned, but saw nothing.

It didn't matter. *This.* This was what really mattered.

Chapter Twenty-Seven

Anna

"Walk with me," Leo said to Anna as he headed toward his car. Even though it was time for him to head back, she was glad that he'd made the trip out. She caught up and matched his pace. But he said nothing. He just marched toward the car. Shmuel held the door open for him.

Once they arrived at the car, Leo nodded, and Shmuel left them and entered the car. The engine was already running.

Leo draped over the open door and still said nothing.

"Pleasant talk," she said. "We should do this more often."

A grin crept onto his face, and then his eyes finally landed on hers.

"What's the chaos that has entered your mind?" she asked.

"Aram. He warned me. About the situation with Cat."

"The press?"

He nodded.

"It's not a coincidence."

"I suspect you're right. They had forgotten me for the last couple of months. Now, out of nowhere... This has Adela written all over it."

Anna placed her hand on his. "Don't even think of approaching her."

His eyes widened. "What makes you say that?"

"Because I know you. You probably think that by speaking to her, she'll pull back the dogs. These paparazzi are not her people. It's not even her scene. What she has done is place a well-informed person to whisper sweet nothings into the ears of the right—or wrong—people. She has released the hounds, but she doesn't control them."

His shoulders slumped. "So all I would do is give her the joy of humbling myself to a terrorist by requesting an audience with her, but she would deny it, and the craziness would continue."

"You got it. Once the privacy is up, it'll be easier."

"Any other ideas?" His eyes were downcast, because he knew that if she had one, she would've already implemented it.

"No. Not yet."

Footsteps approached them. It was Cat.

"When will you be back?" Cat asked Leo.

"Not sure. I'll be fairly busy on multiple business trips over the next couple of weeks."

Cat's eyes visibly went sad.

"But right after, I'll try to spend some quality time here. For a few days at least."

She offered a faint smile. "You'll be missed. Come here. Give me a hug."

He did.

Anna scanned the streets, the sand dunes, and anything that was around them. She knew that all these moments were opportunities for the paparazzi to hound him.

Any other time, none of this would matter. She had actually seen Leo buy a dozen cups of coffee and hand it out to the paparazzi that followed him around.

But now was not a good time. It made him look like a loose cannon to the partners. And it made Cat look unfocused to the court. This was an absolute lose-lose.

Anna had just returned from a nighttime walk along the beach when she saw Van, once again parking his car in that curious angle. This time, when he pulled out the sleeping bag, he winced.

Without hesitation, she walked up to him, grabbed his sleeping bag, and tossed it in his trunk.

He stared at her. "What are you doing?"

"You're not sleeping in the car," she said.

"I'm not?"

"Nope," she said, and faced him. "You'll stay in my RV."

He shook his head. "No. It's best I stay in the car. Only two more nights, and security will be in place."

"Perfect. For the next two nights, you'll make use of the sofa bed in my RV."

He broke eye contact. "Look, I snore."

"Believe me, I remember."

He grinned. "I don't want to put you in an awkward situation."

"Awkward how? With whom?"

"With yourself."

She frowned. "What are you talking about?"

He glanced around, then homed in on her eyes. "I see you reading the Bible. I see you pray before you eat a meal. I get that demarcation line."

She smiled. "Demarcation line?"

"Yeah...you don't come across as someone who... How do you say it?"

She crossed her arms. "Not sure. But I'm looking forward to hearing it."

He put up his hands. "Listen, your faith isn't something that you put on a poster. From what I've seen, you live it out."

She blinked.

"This is real to you. I want to respect that line."

"Van, you continue to surprise me." In her heart, she really wanted to say that he impressed her. But she held back. "The fact that you recognize all of this gives me further confidence in my decision. My conscience is clean. I am helping the person who's helping me and my friends. That's all it is."

He studied her eyes. "You sure?"

She flicked her head toward the RV. "Let's go."

He followed her.

"By the way," she said, "the boss gave me the okay to get one more travel trailer. It'll have two rooms, like Cat's. One for you and one for him when he visits."

"This is starting to feel like a full-time gig."

She opened the door. "Once you're in Leo's webbing, there is no getting out."

"Never said I wanted out." He grinned, and the way his blue eyes lit up... She reminded herself of the demarcation line.

Chapter Twenty-Eight

Catalina

A week later, an entire security system was in place around Casa Moncrieff. Even some aspects of construction had started.

Although José was still working on permits for downstream work, nothing prevented them from removing and hardening the parts that the fire had affected. It was slow going for now, but progress was being made.

Most importantly, after a few failed scheduling attempts, she would see Chicho again. She'd been frustrated that the Rocas had produced one excuse after another to delay things. But today was the day.

Cat had just sat down in the family waiting room when the door opened. She rose quickly, hardly believing her luck that they had already brought him in.

Chicho walked through the door, smiling.

But her smile faltered. His hair. All his beautiful hair was cut short and tight. When they first took him, his hair had longish strands that she would hand brush out of his eyes or tuck behind his ears. When the wind picked up, his hair danced. The first time she saw him, it had grown out quite a bit.

Now, his sides were nearly skintight, and the top was a patch—a hint of hair. They had made him to look like his father.

"Hi, Momma," he said, but did not run to her.

She met him halfway and brought him into a tight hug. It's not that he didn't hug back; it's that something was missing.

"I missed you, Chicho," she said. "How are you?"

"I'm good," he said and gave her the smile that she'd always known and loved.

At least not all was different.

They sat at the table, and as they caught up, he drew. Once again, his natural art talent had improved during the gap in time. He was growing up, and she was not there to witness it. She needed to have him with her.

"I love how well you draw," she said.

"Thanks. You can keep this one." He slid the drawing toward her.

She pulled it closer to her, but did not take her eyes off of him.

"I like your hairstyle," she finally forced out.

He beamed, then touched the sides of his skull. "Touch it, Mom. It feels so cool."

"I bet it does." She ran her hands on both sides.

His beautiful skin was so smooth and tight. A perfect child.

"Do you know what car I drove today?" she asked.

He shook his head. "Mister Lionel's truck?"

"Nope. I came with Leo's spaceship."

His eyes went wide. "Really? Is he here now?"

She shook her head. "No, he's at his other home. But he can't wait to see you again. He misses you."

He smiled. "I miss him, too."

The short time she had with him passed too quickly. As they walked to the door where Maggie would take him back to the family, Cat knelt in front of him.

"Will you pray for me today?" she asked.

"I pray for you every day."

She nearly cried, picturing her perfect little man with hands clasped, eyes closed, asking God to help his mom.

"Thank you," she said. "This one's an important prayer."

"Okay."

"I will ask the judge to let you stay with me, too. Some days with me, some days with Grandma."

He gave her a toothy smile. "That will be awesome. Maybe ask the judge if you can move in with us in Great Grandma's mansion."

Her smile faltered. "Maybe," she whispered. "Give me a hug."

He did, and as they parted, she said, "I love you, Chicho."

He blinked in quick succession. "I love you too. But...um, Mama. I don't want you to call me that anymore."

She frowned. "What?"

"Chicho. Call me Francisco. Grandma says that people should use their real names."

She nodded. She could not form words at that moment. They were changing him. Physically and emotionally.

Zareh was on fire. Cat's attorney laid out the case as well as she could've dreamt. A few times she glanced behind her at Anna and Van to check if they were seeing the awesomeness that was her lawyer.

He provided pictures of the trailer, calling it their temporary home, and the room that had been prepared for Chicho. He presented select information on the construction that was to take place and the vision of what the house would look like. He also gave the court detailed pro forma profit-and-loss statements for the bed-and-breakfast venture. Anna had taken what Cat had built and given it a corporate facelift. Cat had a lot to learn from Anna.

Her attorney showed that she also had the backing of her business partner, Leo. Finally, her therapist's assessment had been nothing but stellar.

When he finished, deep down, she hoped Judge McAuliffe would shock them all and give her full custody and put this behind them once and for all.

Why not? What they were presenting was powerful.

The judge wrote a few things in silence. He set down his pen, pulled off his glasses, and turned to the opposing side.

"What do you have to offer?" he asked.

If she didn't know better, she'd say he looked frustrated. He probably didn't expect that Cat would be so far advanced.

"Your Honor, this is a delightful story they have laid out," their attorney said. "But it is all Hollywood magic."

Cat spun her chair toward him. *What's in their water bottle?*

"Let's establish the facts, Your Honor. It is a fact that her therapist has given Miss Marceli a clean bill of health. The family is relieved beyond measure to hear this. Ideally, we could have her evaluated by our expert therapist, but so far, that request has been denied."

She wanted to correct him that she no longer used that last name, but she held back. She also wanted to call cap on all that 'relieved beyond measure' business. They would've been breaking out champagne bottles if she had landed in an institution instead.

"However," he continued, "that's where the facts take a different turn. Let's start with the housing situation. A mobile home. No, not in a trailer park, but not too far off, either. That's what she's proposing for this young man who has markings of PTSD because of the negligence exhibited leading up to the fire."

"Your Honor," Zareh Maroutian said. "Is that really necessary? Is there any evidence of PTSD? And what negligence? These are inflammatory words, Your Honor."

"Agreed," the judge said. "Counselor, if you have evidence, present it, but I would appreciate it if you stay away from the theatrics. There are no jury members here. So stick to the facts."

Wow, she thought. *He's finally coming around.*

"My apologies, Your Honor," their attorney said. "But there is a reason the family is outraged. Young Francisco is living in a home that 99.99 percent of the population would kill for. And they propose moving him into a mobile home? Furthermore, why, if it's such a good idea, is the house fenced like it's a prison he's moving into? Guards, Your Honor, walk the perimeter. Who are they keeping out? Or do they want to make sure no one leaves?"

Zareh glanced at her and nodded. A non-verbal cue they could not explain the reason for the guards, otherwise risk opening another can of worms—the paparazzi and thieves on the grounds.

"And why all that security, Your Honor? Because the press has gotten wind that Miss Marceli is in a relationship with a flamboyant billionaire who has a history of questionable behavior. From partying irresponsibly, to drinking excessively, to much more. This is a matter of public record."

Zareh interjected. "Your Honor, this public record that the council is referring to are paparazzi rags where they take a picture out of context and make sensational stories to sell papers at the market or sell advertising clicks online. These same sources assure us Elvis is alive. Having said that, it does make us wonder why the paparazzi suddenly took an interest in this man who is an inventor and one of the most respected young minds in the industry. Why now, we ask, after not caring about him for months?"

The judge glared at him. "Are you accusing the family of something, Mr. Maroutian? If you are, you better be ready to produce evidence. It seems you two have watched too many courtroom TV dramas. Evidence, or keep your conspiracy theories to yourself." The judge nodded for the other attorney to continue.

"Your Honor," the other attorney said, "Miss Marceli shows us impressive imaginary money being made by a non-existing business. We are told she has a partner, but it's the same man who has been seen with her romantically. We are assured that she is financially secure, but if not for, once again, the Moncrieff generosity, she has nothing. Even her trailer home, Your Honor, was bought by a company associated with Mr. Moncrieff."

She felt her face drain of all blood.

"In other words, she has nothing that is of her own making. Nothing. She is being propped up to confuse the court and put this child in the hands of someone who, through deception, has created a very nice story. This is Hollywood, through and through. None of it real. But the child is. And if there's more to the fire than meets the eye, then we have to take a very long pause on all of this. We must assure the welfare of the child."

Chapter Twenty-Nine

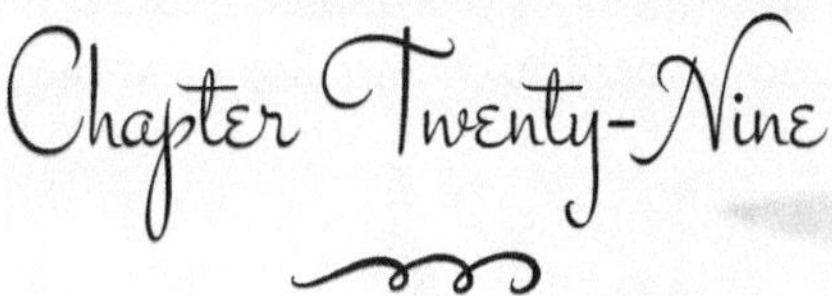

Leo

*D*enied.

That word kept ringing in his ears. Denied. Cat's attempt at achieving partial temporary custody had fallen apart in a hot minute. And based on what Anna had shared, some—most—of the blame was pointed right back at Cat's association with Leo.

To his driver's great concern, Leo had taken the Ferrari for this trip. The chopper had been an option, but he needed time to sort out his thoughts. Also, he had to blow off some steam, and nothing was better at that than the Spider convertible.

What was clear to him was that he had to explain and apologize in person. Although this was possibly the worst time for him to pull away from the project, he also knew that this was the worst time for Cat. This one needed to be done face-to-face.

As he passed the overhead sign that declared Welcome to Fortuny Bay, he thought of another time, maybe a couple of years ago. The same road, the same car. But a completely different set of circumstances. This time, he was not going back home to spar with his father, to show him he had become a success. Instead, he was going to the person he loved.

No, it was not hard for him to declare how he felt about her. He had told her once before, when they were kids. And after all these years, one thing was certain—his love for her had grown. Exponentially.

So he would do this in person. Apologize for his role—small and large —in how the court had determined the outcome.

He turned on the street and was pleased with the security gate he saw. The gate opened automatically. As he pulled onto the property, the guard waved.

He saw the new travel trailer that was being used by Van, and by him too next time he stayed overnight. But that was not what he was looking for. He took a deep breath, then stepped out of the car. He knocked on her door, called out her name, then ventured inside.

Not here.

He walked toward the main house. There were large metal trash bins with the emblem of environmental agencies on them. He was about to enter the house when something told him that's wasn't where he'd find her. He turned around and walked to the beach.

He was a good fifty yards away when he saw her. Cat faced the ocean, seated in the sand, arms wrapped around her bare legs. She was seemingly lost in thought. She wore a sweater he recalled from many, many years ago. His Stanford sweater.

Before he reached her, he slipped off his shoes, stuffed the socks inside them, then buried his feet in the cooling sand. The late afternoon breeze was already chilling down everything.

When he reached her, he stopped for a moment. Without even turning to him, she tapped the spot next to her. He wasn't as ninja as he liked to believe. He released the air he'd been holding and sat down. He mirrored her pose and watched the breaking surf. They remained silent for what seemed an eternity.

"You heard?" she asked.

"I did," he said.

"You paid for my trailer?"

"I did."

Silence.

"Why?" she asked.

"The insurance would play games and shortchange you on everything. I wanted you to have a good place for you and Chicho. Also—"

She laid her hand on his arm. "You misunderstand my question. Why didn't you tell me the truth?"

That was a different question altogether. A question that was not as clean. He decided to try the truth.

"Maybe because I wanted to fight back. I wanted to show that family that you also had resources. I could not let them force you into a suboptimal situation. That family wanted you to live like a homeless person. I would not let them win. So I decided I would take charge and keep you out of it. You would focus on Chicho. I would fight off the barbarians at the gate."

She faced him and stared into his eyes. "By keeping me in the dark, you allowed those same barbarians to undercut me. My lawyer was not prepared to fight back because we didn't know. Thank you for doing what you thought was the right thing. But lying to me, even if you know I'm wrong, is not the way to get things done. You can't do that again."

He nodded. "I understand. But there is some culpability on you also."

Her eyes narrowed. "How do you figure?"

"You called me recently and told me to be your business partner. That's all good and nice. But that's not enough. Not for me. Not anymore. So, as much as what happened sucks, you need to know that if I think something will help you and Chicho, then I will do it. I promise to you I will not keep it a secret from you, but you need to give me that space to be there for you." He laid his hand on her cheek. "I want to help you. I want to fight for you. I want to partner with you in everything." He blinked, took a deep breath, then spoke. "I mean everything."

One brow rose. But she said nothing.

"Do you understand what I'm saying?" he asked.

Her eyes relaxed, and her lips loosened.

He wanted to avoid them. He wanted to focus on her, on the conversation, on the message he wanted to give her. But instead, gravity won, and his lips found hers.

She did not resist; she did not fight him off. She accepted his lips with hers. A connection that he remembered as perfection. A connection that he could not find with anyone else, ever. A melody, an orchestration that no human could design without divine intervention.

The waves cheered them on. The breeze caressed them. All of nature celebrated.

As she pulled back, their lips resisted the movement until it was over. They leaned against each other—shoulder to shoulder, forehead on forehead. And time elapsed.

"I was supposed to yell at you," she said. "You totally messed that up."

"It's a gift."

Silence.

"The time will come," she whispered. "But now is not the time."

He turned to face her, and she mirrored him. They were face-to-face. He recalled this same pose many, many years ago. The day that he broke the news to her that he was leaving without her.

"I'm here for the long run," he said. "I'm here for you. And I will be whoever and whatever you need until we make you whole and complete."

A small smile appeared on her lips.

"Do you believe me when I say that I am not leaving your side? Not again."

She nodded. "I believe you."

They both lay down on the sand, facing each other. He shifted his gaze to the school emblem on her sweater.

"Nice drip," he said.

She studied him and ran her fingers across his jaw. "It was here, on this beach, maybe in this very spot, when you told me you were leaving."

The memory of that day dug into his chest. He did not want to relive that day. He did not want her to remember how shallow he had been.

"Why didn't you tell me you had a fallback plan for college? I would've followed you anywhere."

He swallowed. How he wished he could change the past. But that type of thinking was for children.

"I thought you were disappointed in me when Stanford rejected me," he said. "I felt I had let you down, and that you had finally figured it out."

"Figured what out?" she asked.

"That I was a fraud. I was not that smart. I was not good enough. That one of the finest learning institutions had seen through it all. They had seen the real me through the GPA and standardized test scores, letters of recommendation, and personal letter. They had seen me, finally, for who I really was, not who I wanted to be. And now that the light was cast on me and I was exposed, you had seen it too. In my heart, I thought you would be relieved that I left. That I released you to do whatever you wanted with your life."

She sat up.

He matched her movement and faced her.

"If you had only told me how you felt... If you had been transparent with me, we would've had a different story," she said. "But you know what? I'm glad you did what you did."

His eyes widened.

"You broke my heart, Leo. You threw my life into a spiral that I don't ever want to re-live. But through it all, God was with me. And through it all, He gave me my son. I will go through all of that again and again if it means I'd have Francisco in my life."

He placed his hand on her cheek. She leaned into it and closed her eyes. Warm tears streaked down her cheek.

"No more of that," she said and wiped her face, then gave him a pained smile. "I will get him back. One way or another."

"*We* will get him back."

She nodded.

"Partners?"

"Partners," she confirmed.

They were nearly back at the trailer when he asked a question that had been on his mind since the first day he had come back to Fortuny Bay.

"Cat, why did you hold on to my sweater? Why are you still wearing it after all these years?"

She gave him a look that he did not quite understand. "Your sweater is in your box in the shed."

He frowned. "So...what is this one? Is it yours?"

"Yes."

He stopped. "I don't understand. Why did you get a sweater? I recall, specifically, when I was getting mine as a sign of faith, you would not indulge. You said, and I remember this clearly, that you would not get the sweater until you got accepted."

She said nothing. She just blinked.

The truth came crashing down on him.

"You got in," he said.

She nodded.

"But...why didn't you... I don't understand. If you got in, why did you go to the community college?"

She took a deep breath. "They said no to you. I was going to go wherever you went. So I said no. And by the time you surprised me with your plans..."

He covered his face. "It was too late to attend. You lost your window...

because of me." He dropped his hands, then blinked heavily. "I am so, so sorry, Cat," he whispered.

"Do you know how many times I wanted to call you or message you and tell you? Do you know how righteous I felt? I wanted you to be ashamed and suffer. But each time I wanted to do it, my heart couldn't go through with it. Don't suffer over it now. Look at us. We're almost back to where we were."

He studied her face. How could she look at him? How could she ever forgive him? And yet, here she was. Encouraging him with words that he didn't completely understand, but he could see that her source of goodness came from her faith.

"You know I love you, right?"

Her eyes turned glassy, then red. Tears formed at the edges.

"You don't have to feel the same way I do. But you need to know how—"

She pulled his face into hers and gave him a long, deep kiss then pushed him off.

"We will discuss this at a later time," she said between sniffles.

"Like when? Five minutes? Ten?"

She stormed off and entered her trailer.

He grinned. She hadn't actually said if she loved him too.

But he took that kiss as a solid vote of confidence.

Chapter Thirty

Anna

Anna tapped the table while she waited for the insurance agent on the other side of the call to come back. She looked at the time. Twenty-seven minutes.

Unreal. She would never put up with this type of behavior from the operations arm at their firm.

"Hi, are you still there?" the agent asked.

"Yes, on hold for nearly thirty minutes, but I'm still here."

"Okay, great, thank you for your patience," she said, completely unmoved by Anna's snide comment. "I'm gonna transfer you to my supervisor."

Hallelujah.

The supervisor was marginally more helpful.

"Let me stop you," Anna said after a few minutes of circular conversation. "Here's what I want to know: based on the paperwork I see from previous years, he renewed the home insurance every October."

"That's correct," the supervisor said.

"But the copy of the policy I have in my hand shows a January date. Had there been an October policy in place before this January?"

Silence.

"After all," Anna said, "if the previous year expired at the end of September, Mr. Lionel Moncrieff did not go without home insurance until January, right?"

"Yes...you are right."

"Great. I want to see that policy that was from October."

A few moments later, an email popped up. "Did you get it?"

"Yup," Anna said and opened the attachment. She read it, and her mouth opened. "Okay, so to make sure you and I are on the same page, this policy from October has considerably more coverage than the one we saw in January."

A hesitation. "Yes, it appears so."

"It's not an appearance. It's a fact. Furthermore, every year previous had a similar coverage, correct?"

"Umm, yes, it appears—I mean, yes, it is as you say."

Anna leaned back. "So what happened in January? Do you guys have records of why the policy changed?"

"Like I said, we received a fax with a cover letter asking us to drop the coverage because Mr. Moncrieff could no longer afford the premium."

Anna rose and paced her RV. For a $500 difference per year, she could not believe that Lionel would drop the coverage so drastically.

"Before you guys would speak to me, I had to provide documentation showing that I have a power of attorney. Even though I presented it to you, I still had to jump through hoops."

"We take security and privacy very seriously here," the agent said.

Anna studied the crime wall and focused on Adela. "How did you verify the fax was from Lionel Moncrieff Sr.?"

"Well...it was... The letter had all the details that we would need. So..."

"You didn't know, did you? Did you call him to verify?"

"We sent a revised policy to his home."

She had heard enough. They exchanged a few more words before she ended the call. This was not about getting insurance money to pay for the reconstruction. This was about identifying the crime.

Anna channeled her inner Van. *Assume a crime was committed. How do the details line up now?*

She shifted her gaze to Ricardo Chaparral. A man who visited often. A man who could've intercepted the letter.

An idea dawned on her. She looked up the insurance company. She jumped from one holding company to another until it all came together. The insurance company was owned by Adela Roca.

Unreal.

Two taps on her door and in walked Van.

"Is that Leo's Ferrari outside?"

She hustled to the door and peeked out. She grinned. He had come for Cat. She approved of his chivalry.

Later in the evening, once the four had finished their dinner, they moved onto coffee and dessert. Their conversation centered on the hearing and what was next.

"The judge basically said that he will not grant partial custody at this point," Anna said. "He heard enough to cause him to pause."

"So all we have to do is ease his concerns?" Leo said.

"Easier said than done," Cat said. "They have successfully shown that I can't do anything on my own. Without my patron saints, I am a walking disaster."

"I think we needed to be transparent about it all," Leo said.

"Agreed," Anna said.

"It's not that we were hiding things on purpose, but by not declaring things and being proud of what was happening here, we gave them the upper hand. They were able to make it look unsavory and underhanded," Leo continued.

"So what do you propose?" Cat asked. "It's late now for that, isn't it? They outmaneuvered us."

"Not sure about that," Leo said, then turned to Anna. "We know publications that are friendly to us, don't we?"

Anna smiled. She liked where he was going with this. "A couple of solid ones."

"What if we gave them an exclusive? Give them the entire story. The family history with this home, how it is being restored, the architect who's involved. Be proud of what we're doing. Celebrate it and cut the heart out of the situation they're trying to fabricate. Let them put Cat in a new light. A single mother who has gone through a lot but is now building a home for her and her child. And a home that honors the request of the original owners."

"The house is sort of going from death to life. I would bet that the people would love a resurrection story," Van said.

Anna took a sip of her coffee, then nodded. "This could work. If anything, at least we give Cat a chance to tell her side of the story."

Cat's eyes were downcast. Something was on her mind.

"Thoughts?" Leo asked.

Cat looked at him. "Not sure."

"About what?" he asked.

"About how much I want to tell anyone about the Rocas."

Chapter Thirty-One

Catalina

Cat didn't actually wake up the next morning. She never fell asleep to experience the process of waking up. Instead, she fell deep into thoughts, worries, and anxiety. It was her thoughts, her ideas, her what-ifs that took center stage.

In her vivid imagination, she saw it time and again—she would lose Chicho. And when she wasn't thinking about her son, she thought about Leo and his words. His lips.

At six in the morning, she slid out of bed and forced herself to take a shower. Once finished, try as she might, she had no appetite. Her heart seemed to have expanded in her chest, and her heartbeat overpowered everything else in her body.

She stepped outside and was happy to see that Leo's car was still here. They had convinced him to not go back so late at night. Instead, he would take the three-hour drive to the Mojave Desert for his meetings in the morning.

She walked around the trailer that both Leo and Van were using. She knew his room was the one to the rear. She tapped three times on the window of his room and waited. She tapped again. The shades opened.

If she hadn't been so out of sorts, she would've laughed at his pillow face. Creases and folds had indented lines across his cheeks and forehead. His hair was splattered in multiple directions. And his eyes were barely open.

He slid the window open.

"Sup?" he asked.

"Need to talk before you leave," she said.

He cleared his throat. "Okay." He looked at his wrist, but there was no watch there.

"It's six thirty," she said.

"Give me ten. No, fifteen."

She walked up to his convertible and opened the passenger door. She slid in and was nearly certain she was sitting on the ground, not a chair. She snooped around the center console and only found gum, mints, and a hand sanitizer. She opened the glove compartment and found a variety of things stuffed in there.

Bar coasters with names and numbers on them. Napkins with names and numbers on them. Some with the cliché of all clichés embedded— lipstick lips. Some were yellow and brittle.

She dug her hand in and pulled out more things. Some items fell to the floor. She found parking tickets, a speeding ticket, and—she nearly gasped —what could've been a ladys' underwear. Or maybe swim bottoms. Or possibly dental floss. She did not want to touch it.

She considered shoving it all back in when Leo came outside.

"Let's go get coffee and some croissants from the café and bring it back for the team."

When he opened her door, he saw the junk all over the seat and floor.

"What the—?" He looked surprised. "Hold on," he said, marched back to this trailer then came back with a plastic bag.

He turned the bag inside out, slid his hands into it, and in the same way a dog owner picks up dog poop by using a plastic baggy, Leo collected up the mess from the past and tossed it into the trash bin.

A simple gesture. But the fact that he threw it all away without a second's hesitation—not even a moment to scan them before dumping them—brought a smile to her lips.

With an assortment of croissants, Nutella-infused pastries, and high-end coffees in hand, they went back to his car and buckled in.

She still didn't like how low it all was in the car, but when he turned the ignition, the way the car roared was a bit exhilarating. An old memory surfaced.

"Leo," she said, "was that you, in a car like this one a couple of years ago?"

He closed his eyes, traced his forehead with his fingers. "Can't recall."

"No secrets, remember?"

"Possibly. But probably not." He fought the smile that was threatening his lips.

Cat returned his smile. "You actually peeled out in front of the house before you took off. That was so junior high."

"In my defense, I was much younger."

Her eyes widened. "That was two years ago. Two. Not twenty."

He broke eye contact, aggressively pulled his seat belt, and buckled it in. "If you're gonna be rude, I don't see the point in discussing it any further."

He took off, and for the first time in twenty-four hours, she smiled a genuine smile.

"Who was the blonde next to you?" she asked.

"Don't recall."

"Was that her...umm...clothing material in your glove compartment?"

His face turned red. As red as his Ferrari. "No comment."

The moment of levity disappeared quickly, though. The home's poking roofline and the security gate reminded her that all was not good in her life.

He pulled into the property and killed the engine. She placed her hand on his, stopping him from hopping out.

He faced her. "What's going on, Cat? Why are your eyes red?"

"I hope you can hear my heart when I say this," she said. "If I lose Chicho, nothing else matters. Nothing. Not the house, not the bed-and-breakfast." She took in a shallow breath. "Not even us."

"Cat—"

"Nothing else. When I think of us, guilt covers me. I am ashamed to even think about joy and time with you when my baby, my sweet innocent child, is in the hands of that family. Every minute with them is not just a minute away from me. It is an opportunity for them to change him, lie to him, convince him of a different reality. They are altering him. And I cannot think of anything else while that is happening."

She took a breath, then touched his face. "I pray without pause that all of this will come together at some point. But until that happens, I cannot lose myself with you. I could've looked at all those years with Rafa, with his family, as the worst of my life. But what came out of it was Francisco. He is the *only* reason I have kept my sanity. If I lose him, then it means everything was a loss. The abuse will be lifelong, not just a decade-long battle, but until the day I die, I will know that they stole him from me and got away with it."

He nodded. "We have the same goal. I will not give up on getting him back and getting you back. I am here for you and for him. And I will honor the space you need."

She leaned forward, placed a kiss on his cheek, then caressed his face one more time.

Later that morning, thanks to Cat's attorney's persistence, she was scheduled for another visit with her son. Back-to-back visits for the first time ever. She had insisted on this follow-up sessions. She couldn't put her finger on it, but her gut—an overwhelming instinctive rush—told her she had to see her son again.

She waited patiently, hoping that she wouldn't have to swallow yet one more change in her son. Clothing. Hair. Name. What was left?

The door opened, and he ran into her arms.

"Hi, Mama!"

Oh, how she loved his beautiful voice.

"Hello, Ch— Francisco, my love. How are you?"

"Good. I missed you," he said, which brought unparalleled peace into her heart.

"I missed you, too."

Under the watchful eyes of Maggie, they sat on the sofa and talked about the mundane things in life. He told her what his new favorite foods were. She told him how the house construction was coming along.

The session went on without a hitch. Any concern that she had before she saw him drifted away. He was happy, looked healthy, and had not brought up anything that would concern her.

"Soon, we'll be able to be together again," she said.

But he didn't react.

"We now have three of those big house cars on the property," she said and took out her phone to show the one RV and two travel trailers.

"That's cool," he said as he took the phone out of her hand to look at the pictures.

"That one is where you and I will stay until the big house is built again."

He stopped analyzing the photo and handed her the phone.

"Is something wrong, Francisco?"

He looked up at her with his big brown eyes. "Mama, I want to say that I'm happy with Grandma."

She studied his eyes. "I'm really glad to hear that."

He blinked. "We don't have to fight. I'm happy."

She produced a weak smile. One that cost her. "Nobody's fighting, sweetie. We all want what's best for you. All children should be with their parents."

His blinking quickened, and he began to breathe heavily. "I am happy now, Mama."

His eyes turned glassy.

She flicked her gaze up to Maggie, who seemed to be intently analyzing the situation.

Cat turned her attention to Chicho. "Here's what we're gonna do. We will not talk about these things anymore. Instead, I'll give you a big hug, and you'll give me a big hug too, okay?"

He nodded, his eyes impossibly large.

She hugged him, and as he hugged her back, she thought she heard a whimper.

What are they doing to him?

Chicho was gone, and Cat was in Maggie's office waiting for her to return. She needed to restrain herself because if she lost control, she'd start breaking things.

Maggie walked back in and closed the door. "Sorry it took so long." She sat down but did not make eye contact immediately. "So, what's on your mind?"

Cat's jaw nearly dropped. "What's on my mind? Well, for one, I'd like to know what they're doing to him."

Maggie tilted her head. "I don't know what you mean."

Cat shuddered. "Did you not see how he trembled as he explained time and time again, like a robot, that he was happy?"

Maggie just studied her. "What I heard is a nervous child who was unsure how his mom would take the news. All he said is that he's fine. That he's safe. That he's happy."

"No, that's not what *we* heard. We saw a child not say anything about safety. We heard a child repeat a line that he had been trained to say over and over again. I know Chicho. His eyes told me all I needed to know."

Maggie crossed her arms. "First, you need to respect the fact that he wants to be referred to as Francisco. It is a terrible habit to not call him by his preferred name. You need to respect his choices."

This woman can't be real. He's five!

"Second, you're making accusations that are not only unfounded, but can be interpreted as alarmist. So I would recommend that you use more caution with what you say and how you interpret what you see and hear."

Cat watched this woman who had been good to her. Helpful, in fact. But now, she was different. Whether swayed by the rags, or swayed by influence, Cat did not know. What was clear was that it was all slipping away.

As she drove back home, she realized with complete clarity that she could not do this on her own. This battle was growing fast, and the variables were getting harder and harder to track.

She needed help. She needed her partners.

Chapter Thirty-Two

Leo

Cat's words still rang in Leo's ears as he sped southbound toward the private hangar at Edward's Air Force Base. He refused to believe that after all these years, after the unimaginable journey they had both taken, that they were not meant to be together again.

He would make sure, at any cost, that Adela did not win. More than ever, he was committed to fighting that family until Chicho was in the right place.

After three hours, he was less than an hour away from his destination. He pulled into a gas station to fill up. He quickly scanned through his messages and saw a new slew of articles. All of them being particularly harsh with Cat.

Anger rose in his gut. This was getting out of hand.

Great partner you are.

He hesitated at the thought. Over the past couple of days, he had promised her that he would be there with her. That he'd be side by side with her. That they were in this together, that he was her partner. Even during the drive now, he had declared 'at any cost.'

But those were just words. He was leaving her. Yet again.

A voice mail popped up on his phone. From Cat. Somehow, he had missed her call from a couple of hours earlier. He knew she had an appointment to see her son. Maybe she just wanted to let him know how it went.

He hit play and listened to her voicemail.

"Leo, something's happening with Chicho that's worrying me. I need the team to regroup. I need to talk this out with people who can guide me through this mess. And maybe we can come up with a new plan. I know you'll be away, but when you're free, please call me. Please."

When the recording finished, Leo took a deep breath. He scanned around the desert. He had been doing what he had always done. Work. Make money. Pretend to be there for those who loved him by sending them money. But was he actually available to them during their times of need?

At any cost.

He dialed Chris.

"Hey," Chris said. "You almost there?"

"No. Not going," Leo said.

"What?" There was a hint of anger in his tone, not concern. "What do you mean? Everyone will be there. You have to be there. We can't drop the ball."

Leo turned on his engine and revved it. That sound was like a shot of adrenaline.

"We're not dropping the ball. You are representing the company. I am removing myself. I'll advise Aram that for the next six or nine months, I will be an adviser and not a direct participant. My decision is done."

In the silence, Leo could almost hear Chris's brain connecting the pieces.

"So...what does that mean?" Chris asked.

"Simple. You're in charge," Leo said, accelerated the car out of the gas station and headed back toward Fortuny Bay.

"I'm the technical guy. I'm not the leader guy."

"You are now. And everything is technical at this stage, anyway. You'll lead the project. You'll lead the team. So if it goes badly, it's on you. If it goes well, it's on you."

More silence. Then, "But why?"

"Simple, Chris. I need to step up and do what's right. Cat and Chicho need my help. I can't be a spectator from the stands in this. I'm throwing money at this, but they need me. The person. I need to be there with her. I need to show her and myself that I am serious about the future I want. This is *the* most important thing for me."

"Wow. I think I'll insult you if I asked...but I'll ask anyway: you sure about this?"

Leo smiled, and relief filled his lungs. "Absolutely no doubt. I'll call Aram next. Make us proud."

Chapter Thirty-Three

Anna

Anna poured the boiling water over the tea bags for the two mugs that would be needed. Cat had called her minutes ago about what had happened with Chicho and about yet another round of articles. Anna suspected that they'd soon graduate from tea to wine, but this was a good place to start.

The promised email came through. Anna had just opened the link to the article when Cat rushed into her RV.

"Did you see it?" Cat asked.

"Just barely. Sit. I've made us some tea."

Cat slumped onto the sofa. "It's relentless. They are coming after us repeatedly."

"I know," Anna said. "And I don't see it slowing down anytime soon."

But as she spoke those words, she suspected—was practically convinced —that if Cat lost her custody case, then these stories would also end.

"And some of those pictures... They make what we...what we did look so horrible. Even the gates are not enough of a deterrent to these people."

Anna sat down, sliding over one mug to Cat. She looked at the two of them on the beach, kissing. "Clearly, it's not horrible. You guys are picking up where you left off some ten years ago."

Cat dragged a hand across her face. "They're going to use this against me. They'll show that I don't even care about Chicho. They will make the case that I'm more interested in messing around than putting my house in order."

Anna snapped her fingers, bringing Cat out of her state. "And they will do a lot more. We all know this. They will not be fair about this. If in their hearts and minds they believe you are dangerous, they will pull out all the stops. They will go after you with a vengeance."

Cat's eyes widened. Her brows cast downcast. "Just like I would."

Anna shook her head. "Just like you *will*. Do you believe they are not good for Chicho? Do you believe he is worse off? Because if he is better off with them than with you, then we need to have a different conversation."

Cat straightened, her jaw pulsating. "Under no scenario, under no condition, is my Chicho better off with them than me. In fact, I believe— no, I know—that with them, he will suffer over time."

"Then let's schedule the call with the reporter. Let's get your story out there. Let's show them all who you are."

At that instant, the gate opened, and tires crunched on the gravel path. They both stepped outside. She put up her hand to shield her eyes from the glare of the sun.

"That's José and Oscar," Cat said.

What's José doing here?

They hopped out of his truck.

"What brings you here?" Cat asked.

He did not look pleased.

"I wish I was here to share good news," José said. "Unfortunately, I have bad news. They denied our permit."

"What?" Anna asked.

"What do you mean, denied?" Cat asked.

"As planned, we were to demolition the damaged areas, and at the same time address potential risks during the cleanup."

"That's right. This permit was very limited. We're not even trying to pitch the extensions yet," Cat said.

"Correct. That's all we wanted," José said. "However, their inspector said that in his assessment, the house needs to be torn down. Completely. He does not feel the house will be safe."

Oscar chimed in. "Which makes little sense. We have the sign-off from the private engineer. The entire structure has been evaluated and greenlit."

Cat glanced at Anna, then back to José. "What now?"

"We will escalate and get this sorted. No way that this will hold. We'll get it to the county supervisor for an overrule."

Cat's tight shoulders seemed to relax. "Then we'll be okay. You're sure of it, right?"

"No doubt about it," José said. "But that introduces another problem. Because of the backlog, we won't get in front of the supervisor for a good four to six weeks."

Cat remained frozen. "Four to six?"

"Hopefully," José said.

"What can we do in the meantime?" Anna asked, hoping to salvage some of it.

"Honestly?" José said. "Nothing. We're dead in the water."

As much as she hated the thought of leaving Cat alone, Anna and Van had important plans. The games were afoot. They showed up unannounced at Chaparral's office.

"I'm sorry," the receptionist said, "but he's with another client, and then another one is coming right after."

"We won't take more than a minute or two," Anna said. "This is something he will want to hear about."

While they waited, Anna glanced at Van. Like an automated camera taking in a panoramic shot, Van scanned the room left to right, as if his eyes were capturing everything in the office.

Chaparral's door opened, and a client walked out, Chaparral right behind him. When he saw Anna, he blinked, scanned from her to Van, but then quickly recovered and walked the client out of the office.

"Anna. Van. I apologize, but I have another meeting," he said.

"I told them, Ricardo," the receptionist said.

Anna rose. "I think you'll want to know about this. We just need a moment. In private."

Ricardo nodded and gestured to his office. Anna and Van walked in, and Ricardo closed the door.

"We found Lionel Moncrieff's passion project," Anna said.

Ricardo blinked three or four times rapidly. "Oh," he said. "That's fantastic. How? Where?"

"I don't want to get into the details right now, but wanted to see if we can count on you help decode it for us."

He flinched. "Me? I'm not sure how I could be of help."

"Well, some of the material is related to Lionel's customer accounts. Since you were his attorney, and you've been in this town for decades, you may be able to give us some context. Because, to be honest, it is very confusing. Leo has not had a chance yet to study it, but if you can be of help, we'd all appreciate it."

He shrugged. "I doubt I'll be of any value. And if the customers referenced are clients of mine, then I definitely can't."

Anna nodded. "That is too bad. We had hoped that maybe you could help unravel this mess. There are so many intriguing questions."

Ricardo's eyes remained hard and unflinching. "I do apologize."

"If you can't, you can't," Anna said. "We understand. Either way, we thought you'd be glad that at least we now have the content. What it means is a whole different matter."

Ricardo smiled. "If there's nothing else."

They all walked out into the reception area. She did not see another client.

"Say, can I get a document printed while we're here?" Van asked.

Anna stared at him. *What is he up to?*

"Sure, of course." He grabbed a card from the receptionist's desk. "Send it to this email. It'll go to her."

Van typed away and put up his thumb.

"All the best," Ricardo said, then turned to his assistant. "Hold my calls."

He rushed back into his office.

They waited in uncomfortable silence for a handful of seconds while the copier spit out the paper.

"Here you go," the receptionist said as she handed him the two-page document.

They walked out, then rushed to the car.

"What do you think?" she asked.

"His first question was telling. He wanted to know where and how we found it."

"Yup," she said. "You'd think he'd want to know what it is. Isn't that a more interesting question?"

"However, I expected he'd want to help decipher it. If he was the one to hide the original, as we suspect, then he'd have a vested interest to keep close tabs on what we decipher. Or even misdirect us. Based on his reaction, I'm not sure what to make of it. Maybe he's done with all of this, and he's trying to create distance with the Moncrieff and Alonzo families."

Anna had thought the same thing. His reaction surprised her.

Just then, her phone rang. She looked at the name. Ricardo. She showed it to Van, then answered the phone.

"Hi, Ricardo."

"Listen, Anna. I changed my mind. Please bring everything you have on Lionel's passion project. I'll be happy to sift through it and give you guidance."

She smiled. "Thank you. We'll get back to you soon." She hung up and faced Van. "He wants to see the material."

Van turned on the car. "Excellent."

"Why the change of heart?" she asked.

"Maybe he was instructed to change his heart."

She leaned back. "You always find the worst-case scenario."

"I always find the most likely case scenario." He pulled away from the curb. "I'm going to drop you off, then I have to pick up something from a police contact. Also, some guy with a dog may show up. Let him in."

She stared at him. "Are you going to tell me what you're up to?"

"Sure. Eventually."

Chapter Thirty-Four

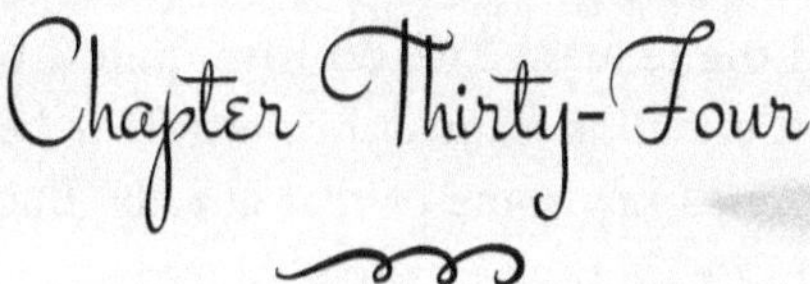

Catalina

Cat paced around the trailer. She was engaged in a combination of a prayer walk and a complaint session. She couldn't wait to talk to Leo. Anna had explained that he was sequestered with no phones and no access to the outside world. Like with all things, Cat would have to wait.

All things are interconnected.

If that were the case, she wondered if the permit agency was also in the mix. José's idea to escalate outside of Fortuny gave her another idea. Was there another path that could completely circumvent the city council?

Days earlier, both José and Pete Nicos had asked about the architect behind the house. Although she had done some cursory research online, she knew she needed to do more. This was as good a time to investigate instead of just wait. It was time to visit the library and dig up some town history.

Minutes later, she entered the library.

"Catalina?" a frail voice called out.

She turned and found the librarian. "Mrs. Palomar?" A face from more than a decade ago. "I should've known you'd still be here."

They embraced.

"Tell me, sweetheart, what brings you here?"

Cat looked over her shoulder, scanned the place, then leaned in. "History of this town. Specifically, about the early days of settlement and construction. I'm looking for names of builders, landowners, and architects who may have worked here."

She considered the request. "We do have quite a bit of that in digital format. The Roca foundation wanted their history to be preserved."

Cat nodded. "Yes, I saw some of that already. But...I want to see the source material. In case...you never know. Maybe some of the content was missed."

The librarian smiled. "Or omitted?"

Cat grinned. This woman was a gem.

"Can you help me?" Cat asked.

She took Cat's hand and walked her toward the basement door. "I can do better than that," she said. "I'll give you the documents that they excluded and told me to remove."

Cat's heartbeat accelerated as they walked down the dusty stairs to a storage area. From one shelf, Mrs. Palomar attempted to pull a box, but it was too heavy for her.

"Let me," Cat said.

"Just take it with you. It's probably safer with you than here."

Twenty minutes later, she was back in her RV, headphones on, reading through articles and yellowed permits. Among the troves were a few pictures of the early settlers.

"There!" she said to herself as she found a picture of the Casa family. She recognized the same faces from the pictures she had found weeks earlier when she was organizing the photos in Lionel's study.

"Who is that?" She touched the face of a lady who had also been in the other pictures.

Again, she was standing in the middle. The Casa family and others were surrounding her. In this particular picture, the mystery woman held a shovel.

Breaking ground.

But who was she?

Ask Pete Nicos, a voice that sounded very much like hers said inside her head.

She set the photo against a dark background and took as clear of a picture as possible. She took pictures of some of the articles and permits, then sent them off to the architect.

She smiled at her work. Maybe it would mount up to something. Maybe it wouldn't.

When she removed her headphones, she heard voices outside. She ran outdoors, hoping that maybe... but no. It was not Leo.

Some guy with a leashed dog stood by his side. Van and Anna were chatting with him.

Cat joined them. "Hi."

They all faced her.

"Oh, good. You're here," Anna said. "I knocked on your door some twenty minutes ago, but you didn't respond."

"Headphones. Sorry about that."

"No problem. Jeff, this is Catalina Alonzo, the owner of the home." She then faced Cat. "Jeff Levine is a private inspector who Van hired."

Cat did a double take. "Inspecting what, exactly?"

"The source of the fire," Van said. "The real source."

Cat tilted her head. "You have my attention."

"Let me show you what I found," he said.

They all walked to the front of the house.

"The city's fire inspector said that they had identified the starting point as the front door. I agree with this assessment. Observing the physical attributes of this scene, and analyzing the physical evidence from the scene, is how we can determine the nature of the fire."

"Nature?" Cat asked.

"Van asked me to determine if the cause of the fire was accidental or deliberate."

Cat blinked heavily. "Deliberate. As in arson."

"That's right." He walked up the steps and pointed to the charred walls. "I was looking for evidence of accelerants, or utilities that were tampered with, and burn patterns that may point me toward a criminal act."

He pointed to a specific burn pattern. "This is what we call a plume. A cone-shaped mark that is produced by the flames which show, among other things, the direction the fire spread and speed of the burn." He pointed to one column. "This is called an alligatoring effect."

The wood was so badly burnt that it looked like it was the tail of a black alligator.

"Notice the other one. The alligatoring effect is minimal. I won't bore you with the things we look for, like the melting point and the ignition temperatures of the materials involved. What I will say is that there is no doubt that this is, in fact, the origin of the fire. So then I had to determine which quadrant did it start in and what evidence, if any, will point me to the cause."

She bit the inside of her cheek. She didn't want this to be arson. Because if it was, then it meant...

"If an accelerant is used, we normally find traces of it in wet floors, carpets, or rags. Having said that, a lot of time has passed. So anything that could've pointed us toward an answer would've evaporated by now."

The dog whimpered.

"That's where my dog comes in." He gave the dog a treat, then petted it. "Once the water drained from this fire, the accelerant used would've evaporated as a plume, and sometimes, in the right condition, the plume will stratify. I trained my sniffer dog to detect them."

He picked up the Welcome mat. "This is what my dog found. Smell this corner here."

She did and immediately pulled back. "Smells like fuel."

Anna and Van also took a whiff.

"The reason it smells like it is because many of the same compounds are found in the accelerant used."

She turned away and sat on the charred step. Someone had tried to burn the house down. Had they known that Chicho and Anna were inside? Blood drained from her face.

"You turned pale," Anna said. "Let me get you water."

"I'm okay," she choked out. "I'll be okay."

"Will you run lab tests?" Van asked.

"Of course. It'll take me a few of days, but I will show, without fear of contradiction, that this was not an electrical fire. This was a deliberate act. This was, in fact—"

"Attempted murder," Cat said.

All eyes turned to her.

"There were two people asleep in this house when they started the fire. Whoever did this either didn't care or was, in fact, intent on doing just that. Burn two people to death."

No one spoke a word. The sound of the wind was the only thing that she could hear. That, and the thudding of her heart against her chest.

Thud. Thud. Thud.

Then Van looked to the sky.

Anna joined him.

Jeff Levine leaned over the awning and looked up as well.

Cat slid off the seat, walked out, and looked up. She had to shield the sun with her hand. But she didn't need to see anything. She could hear it.

A helicopter was landing.

Cat walked toward the spot that the helicopter was about to land on. With each foot that it descended, she picked up her pace. By the time it touched down, she was practically running.

Leo stepped out, closed the door, and slapped it a couple of times. The pilot gave him a thumbs-up. Leo returned the gesture, then turned and rushed toward Cat.

She slammed into his chest and breathed him in deeply. He had been here just hours earlier. And yet, that time away felt like days or weeks had passed. He was not supposed to be here. And yet, here he was.

The helicopter lifted off and flew away.

"Hey, Cat," he whispered. "Not to break up this awesome greeting, but there's a dude and a dog by your house."

She laughed, then grabbed his face and kissed him. How she loved his warmth and the taste of his lips. She needed him. Despite what she said, she knew that when he was around, she operated from confidence.

When she pulled away, she studied his eyes.

He wiped away at the tears that had raced down her cheeks.

"What are you doing here?" she asked. "You were supposed to be sequestered and out of touch and..."

"I decided I have more important work to get to," he said. "I decided that if I'm going to use words like partner, then I need to behave like a partner. So here I am."

She glanced at the sky as the chopper disappeared. "And the grand entrance?"

He shrugged. "Driving would lose me another two hours. Decided I needed quick access back home."

She smiled. "Welcome home. There is much to discuss."

Chapter Thirty-Five

Leo

The four of them gathered in the war room. The fire inspector had already left, and as the details of his preliminary finding were conveyed to Leo, he experienced the gamut of emotions. From shock, to anger, to sadness. Then back to anger.

Then Cat recounted the situation with Chicho. When she finished, his anger level had discovered a new high.

"What I saw in his eyes was fear," Cat said. "Whatever emotions and thoughts they inserted into his heart, it was bad."

"So..." Leo said, "we now know that the fire was not accidental. It may have been a warning shot that got out of hand. Or it may have been planned to be something much worse."

"We also know that the house insurance modification was also an inside job. Furthermore, the paparazzi were used to derail Cat's court hearing and to ruin you professionally," Anna said. "Two more coincidences to add to the growing list."

"We also know that Chaparral is sus," Van said. "Your father did not trust him. And he must've known more about your father's secret project.

He wanted to distance himself from us and the material, but minutes later, he wanted back in."

"You think he was told to stay close?" Leo asked.

"Wouldn't surprise me. He's done their bidding before."

Leo studied him. "What are you referring to?"

Van pulled two folders. One was labeled News Clippings. He spread them out on the table. They were the ones that had been left on Leo's windshield the night of the fire.

"You think he put these on my car?"

"Someone in the office at least," Van said, then pulled two pages from the other folder. "I asked Chaparral's receptionist to print out something I needed. Look at these." He laid the pages next to the news articles. He pointed to a faint line that could be seen every other page. "Copier's drum needs to be replaced or at a minimum cleaned. It's not DNA evidence, but pretty darn coincidental."

Leo glanced at Cat, whose mouth was partially open.

"I can't even..." she said. "I could see him throwing me to the side. Fine. But he was your dad's friend."

"Maybe he was. Maybe he wasn't," Leo said. "It's clear, at least to me, that we've been operating against something much wider than we expected. Clearly, others are involved."

"There's one more thing," Van said.

"I'm afraid to ask," Leo said.

Van grabbed the laptop and uploaded something onto it. He turned the laptop around so the rest of them could see it. On the screen was a video from an unfamiliar home's door camera. He paused it on a fairly decent color image of a street. No cars in the view, just the houses across the street.

"As you know, we've been tracking various threads," Van said. "One of them had been around your father's illness and why the treatments did not work and so on."

Leo gave him a curt nod. "You found something?"

"I did. The nurse, the only nurse who tended to Mr. Lionel Moncrieff, died in a hit-and-run accident. The newspapers never followed up on what happened to the driver. But I had my contacts look into it. The man behind the accident is at large. But it turns out a house across the street had a door camera. Therefore, it caught a partial license plate and revealed that the driver was a man.

"They tracked the car down to one that had been stolen an hour or so earlier. They have not identified the man. More on that in a bit. But one thing is for sure, at least to me. This was no accident." He pressed the space bar, which started the video.

They all leaned in, but Van remained standing, arms crossed. The camera's view was at a slight angle, such that you could see the house across the street and a few more to its left.

From the right side, a woman in sweats came into view, running on the street. The quality was good enough that Leo could see white headphone cables dangling. A second into it, and she had passed the house directly in front of the camera, passed the next one, and was at the third house. Her orientation was no longer sideways, but instead, her back was to the camera.

Suddenly, from the right, a car showed up, and slammed into her then took off.

"Oh no," Anna said.

"Did he aim for her?" Leo asked.

"Play it again," Cat said.

He did. It was hard to believe, but it seemed like the car turned toward her. Made a beeline directly toward her.

"It was no accident," Van said again. "This was deliberate."

"Murder?" Cat asked.

"In my opinion, yes," Van said.

"What did the police say?" Leo asked.

"They seem to think I'm reading into it. Because the road curves, they say it creates the impression that he's aiming toward her. Bottom line, they don't want to go after it."

"But why wouldn't they?" Cat asked.

"With all due respect, Miss Alonzo, for me, there are two questions we need to answer. First question: why was the nurse targeted?"

They all became silent.

"You don't think this was just some sick criminal who was mentally unwell? In other words, you don't believe this was a random crime. You think this was planned?" As Anna said those words, Leo felt a cold chill.

"I do." Van zoomed in on the grainy image of the bald driver. "This leads to the second question. Who is he?"

"Do you know?" Leo asked.

"No. Not yet. But if I'm not wrong, he has visited us here recently."

"What?" Cat and Anna asked simultaneously.

Van brought up another image. "The night after the lumber was stolen, I placed a small, low quality camera facing the street." He showed a zoomed-in and enhanced image of a bald man, looking over his shoulder toward the house. "Hard to know for sure. But the thick neck and bald head are very similar to the hit-and-run suspect."

Van put both still images side by side.

Leo leaned in, looking from one image to the other. "If I were a betting man, I'd say we have a big problem on our hands. Are Cat and Anna safe here?"

Van nodded. "We have armed security and we have perimeter fencing. We still have to be careful. But here, it's safe. But the stakes are clearly much higher than we initially thought."

Leo blinked. "We need a new plan. I want answers."

Chapter Thirty-Six

Anna

The sun had already set. Leftover pizza, Chinese takeout, and air-fried chicken strips had been devoured, and more than a healthy amount of beer and wine had washed it all down.

It was a clear night. No fog, no obstruction. The full moon's face was lighting up the entire property down to the ocean.

The pause had been good for them. But work needed to be done. They all went back into Anna's RV to regroup.

"I've been thinking about the enemy we're going up against," Leo said. "I had assumed that because I have resources, I could fight them blow for blow. But that's not how this one has gone."

"Because you're not playing the same game," Van said.

They all faced him.

"No?" Anna asked.

Van shook his head. "You're trying to win the case. You're trying to bring back Francisco home to his mother. You'll do whatever you can to win—get the best lawyer, show evidence, make the case, use logic. But that will not work with them."

"Why's that?" Cat asked.

"I start with the assumption a crime has been committed. A crime is perpetrated by a criminal. There are various types of criminals, but let's simplify it down to two types. The one who commits a crime in the process of getting what they want. And the one who is a criminal. One is the act. The other is an embodiment. If I'm right, then that family looks at crime not as a necessary tool to get what they want. Instead, crime is the currency they trade in."

They all breathed out.

"This is insane. It's like we're going up against Goliath," Anna said. "If what you say is true, then that means we're not equipped to play their game. We're trying to win with the law. But if...if they are merchants of crime, then they will use and do anything to win."

"Goliath," Leo said.

Anna glanced at him. "Do we throw more lawyers?"

"Goliath," Leo repeated.

"Something on your mind, Leo?" Cat asked.

"Yeah. Work this out with me. I'm a bit drunk, so help me out. Goliath lost because of the little guy—"

"David," Van inserted.

"Yeah, David, that's right. Because he shot that little stone at exactly the right spot to bring him down. The big dude was all armored up, right?"

"He was," Anna said.

"But he found the weakness. Like that other dude," he said, now flaying his hands around, pointing at nothing in particular. His words were coming out in rapid fire now. "The Achilles-heel situation. They knew the weakness and went after it. That's what we need. The weak spot. We can't just attack with what we've done. We need to find the soft, fleshy part."

"I like where you're going with this," Van said.

"Let's take a look at the crime wall," Leo said.

"Crime wall?" Cat asked.

Van pulled off the panels, showing the state of the investigation.

Cat breathed out. Her eyes turned glassy. For a moment, Anna thought she would break down, but instead she clenched her fists.

"Walk me through this," Cat said. "What does it show, and what do we know?"

"We started with a basic theory," Anna said. "Everything is interconnected. There are no coincidences. And a crime, or crimes, has been perpetuated against Lionel, you, and Francisco."

"We looked at everything through that lens," Van added.

"Chaparral is at the center," Cat said. "Does the position on the wall mean anything?"

"Just that a lot of the interconnections have gone through him," Anna said. "The original will, the new will, the sale of the house, the insurance, the missing passion project documents, and representing Chicho. What we suspect is that he's deeply involved, but he doesn't want to be. They have something on him."

"Then we have a nurse who was the single point of direct care for Lionel, and she was murdered," Van said.

"We don't know that for sure," Leo added.

"We don't know anything for sure," Anna said. "But we're making the connections. The same guy in the video seems to be the same guy who drove by this property. No coincidences, remember?"

He nodded.

"We know that someone tried to burn Casa Moncrieff down," Anna said. "No doubt in that. And that the fire inspector created a highly questionable report. In fact, I almost feel like he used childish explanations on purpose. Almost to call out the questionability of his report."

"I hate to ask," Leo said, "but since he's still missing, do we suspect foul play?"

Van shrugged. "Either that, or he knows who he's dealing with and wants to hide away until, hopefully, the truth emerges or it all dies down. I contacted people I know, and there is no evidence that he's rented a car, taken a flight, or crossed borders to the north or south."

"Then there's the house," Cat said. "The rejection of the permits stinks of the Rocas putting pressure."

"What about the judge?" Leo asked. "Is he clean?"

"I know this will sound like a cliché," Anna said, "but it is a fact that organized crime of any sort needs the law and the justice system on their side in order to have sustained success."

"Man, this is insane. What do we really know of the Rocas?" Leo asked.

A momentary hesitation, and they all faced Cat.

She nodded. "It's time. I guess it's as good a time as any."

Chapter Thirty-Seven

Catalina

Cat brought her laptop and connected it to Anna's TV. The work she had done so far to document what she knew and had discovered of the Roca empire was as good as ready to show this group.

"Adela Roca is the head of the empire," Cat said as she opened up a file with her photo in the center. "Her husband passed away right at the same time that you left Fortuny Bay, Leo."

"So, he dies. She takes over," Leo said. "I wonder if the business grew right after his death."

"It did," Cat said, flipping to another page showing the map of the city. All over the map were various check marks. "The green are those that I know they own. The yellow I suspect they own or have an interest, because from what I could tell, the lender was Roca Community Bank."

"Those are a lot of check marks," Van said.

"At least half, I'd say. I wonder about home loans," Anna added.

Cat flipped a few slides forward. "A lot of those, too."

"Somebody has been dusting off her research skills and killing it," Leo said. "Again, a lot of home loans under the control of the Rocas."

"After her husband died is when the realty company, the bank, and the insurance broker showed up. So, yes, the business grew and presumably the profits." Cat flipped back to an earlier slide. "So Adela at the top. She has three kids. One son, Ferdinand, runs the Mexico operation of their fishing business. The other son, Manuel, runs the San Diego area fishing business. And her daughter, Elizabeta Roca Marceli, runs the Fortuny Bay business."

"What about Elizabeta's husband?" Van asked. "Does he have a role?"

Cat smiled. "He died some six years ago when I was still with Rafa. He was actually a fairly decent guy."

Leo sat up. "Natural causes?"

Cat shrugged. "So they said. To me, he was healthy as a mule."

"I'm no child genius like the boss here, but I'm seeing a pattern," Van said.

Anna blew out a slow, steady breath. "And Rafa's involvement?"

"He was in charge of business development," Cat said.

Leo laughed, then quickly controlled himself. "Sorry, sorry. But business development? What does that mean? Work out trade routes with the sardines?"

"Whatever it was, I personally saw him bring in duffel bags of cash on more than one occasion. I was not supposed to have seen that, but I did."

They all stared at Cat.

"Drugs?" Van asked.

"Is that what that ship and boat are doing? Bringing in drugs?"

Cat leaned against the wall. "I don't know. I really don't."

Leo rose, grabbed his father's client ledger, and started flipping through it. "I wonder."

"What's going on in that brain of yours?" Anna asked.

"The classic saying of maintaining two books. One is what is audited. The other is the truth. I wonder if my dad picked up on something with these various clients that didn't sound right."

Cat opened up a spreadsheet with names of businesses that the Rocas owned or owned the loan. "Read me some of the names."

"The café?" he asked.

"Yup."

"Barb, the waitress there, told me how much everyone stressed each time Adela walked in. How about Harvey's Barbecue?"

"The place that gave us all an odd look," Anna said.

"On the list."

Each one that Leo read was on her list.

"How about Andy's Burger and Shakes?" Leo asked.

"Nope. Are they on your dad's list?"

"No. Which is why I asked. When I first came here, you and I went there. They were kind to you and super friendly. So I suspect now that this is because they were not under the Roca thumb."

Cat highlighted another one. "Chaparral is on the list."

"Not surprising," Van said.

Leo set the book down and sat back on the chair. "Without the filings for these companies at hand, I'm going to make a guess. The income they produced did not match the business operations. And these people cannot say anything because their entire livelihood depends on the Roca family."

"Do we need to prove it?" Anna asked.

They all faced her.

"My point is, all we need to do is give a governmental agency enough for them to do the work. I would bet Leo's Ferrari that the Rocas are already under a watchful eye of the IRS or the FBI. When Rafa died, questions were raised. Those questions must've gotten the attention of the attorney general."

"She makes a good point," Van said. "I don't have connections in those areas. Otherwise—"

"I do," Leo said. "I definitely do. Let's see if I can poke the bear." He faced Cat. "What happened with Rafa? Was it just a simple boating accident, or do you think there was more to it?"

Cat tapped her fingers against the table, buying some time.

"Let's be honest," Anna said, "the men in the Roca and Marceli lines don't have a very long life span. So, there's that..."

"I don't believe what I went through with that family is relevant," Cat said. "But I will share with you what I refused to discuss, even during my trial. I need to explain to you how Rafa died, but I don't want any of this to get to Chicho. He does not need to know. Ever. Agreed?"

"Of course," Leo said, and that was good enough for her.

"Rafa and his family started out nice enough. But when I couldn't get pregnant immediately post wedding, things changed. I saw their true colors. I won't get into the comments, the daily torment, the finger pointing, the threats of finding a real woman, and so on. That was my life for the first three years. Then I got pregnant.

"A big celebration. But then back to the same. In fact, they took over. They were the ones raising the child. I would seldom hold him.

"When Chicho was barely six months old, Rafa changed. Stressed.

Angry. Short. Often very paranoid. The business was evolving, is what he once said. Sometimes, he'd leave on business trips for weeks on end. He'd come back angry, uninterested. So much so that he even got into it with his own mother a couple of times."

"Do you know the nature of the business evolution?" Anna asked.

"No. No clue. It could've been that he just wanted to expand the business," Cat said, "but he wouldn't tell me. One night, he came home drunk. He got mad at me over something. He was about to hit... Anyway, he lost his footing and fell down the stairs and broke his hip."

"Hold up," Van said. "Did he try to hit you?"

Leo's eyes narrowed. His body seemed to tighten.

Cat would not go down that rabbit hole. "It's irrelevant. He fell. He was badly hurt. He blamed me. As did the rest of the family. They placed him on Oxycodone. He was always in pain, so he kept adding more and more to his dosage. Instead of five to seven per day, he was nearing eight to ten."

"Oh crap," Van said. "Wait. Was he all jacked up on that the night of the accident?"

"There's more," she said. "I was going through a lot at this stage as well. Emotionally, physically... I was given Ativan."

"Ativan is what?" Leo asked.

"Sleeping and anti-anxiety," Van said.

"That's right," Cat said. "After they found his body, the coroner confirmed excessive dosage of Oxy. But also, a significant amount of Ativan."

"He took your pills?" Van asked.

She shrugged. "That was the claim. By the time the police came, my meds were all gone. Empty jar. I know I didn't take them. That's when I was convinced that they were setting me up. So the narrative became that I gave him the pills knowing that the combination of Ativan and Oxy were deadly. Particularly when he fell into the water. He would not have survived the cold. His heart would've given up. And that's exactly what happened."

Silence.

"He went on a solo ride during a weather warning. Does that make sense to anyone else?" Anna asked.

"Nope," Van said. "Unless he had to do something that could not wait."

Cat considered the words she was about to speak carefully. If not now, when?

"Between us," she said, "I don't believe he went alone. He never had. He was not very good at captaining the yacht. In those conditions, particularly... I never believed it. But no one ever believed me, either."

Chapter Thirty-Eight

Leo

Leo took a deep breath and then exhaled. "Well...I suddenly feel so much better about having security around the property."

They all chuckled. But the anxiety in the air was thick.

"We need a plan of attack," he said.

Anna grabbed a dry-erase marker and went to the whiteboard.

"Our biggest issue right now is the court hearings," Leo said. "Cat, I hate to say this, but we may want to slow things down a bit so that we can line up the dominos."

"I think that's a good idea," Van said. "I have a couple of things in the hopper that might shed some light."

They all turned to him.

"Go on. Spill the beans," Leo said.

Van ran his hand over his hair. "Earlier, I showed you the printouts from Chaparral's copier. When we were there, I emailed his assistant a file for her to open and print."

"Dude," Leo said. "Was it a hot file?"

He nodded.

Leo grinned. "Brilliant."

"Someone explain," Cat said.

"The file launched a worm on the assistant's computer," Anna said.

"And the worm will give us an in on her computer," Leo said.

"Better than that. A friend who shall remain nameless used this same script with the NSA to track and capture terrorist cells in Madrid. What it does is that it actively branches out to any email recipient and gives us an inside view into the connections and conversations."

Cat's eyes were wide open. "So you're saying if we can show some shady business, we can use it to get Chicho back?"

"No," Van said. "What I've done is illegal. Not admissible in any way, shape or form."

"Then what? Information?" she asked.

"Exactly. We will know for sure and we may be able to whisper information to law enforcement. Something to the effect of if you look here, you'll find that."

Cat rose, walked over to the wine rack, and pulled a bottle and an opener. Anna grabbed glasses.

After pouring each a glass, they lifted them.

"To turning the tables on the Rocas," Cat said.

They all drank some, then set the glasses on the table.

"So, we will get insight on Roberto," Anna said, and scribbled it down. "That may lead us to internal conversations with any of the Rocas or generals of theirs."

"Right," Van said.

"We also need to track the financial movements of this town," Anna said. "To see if there are indeed shady transactions going on."

"I'll take that one," Leo said. He rose, took off his jacket, and tossed it on the couch. "If anyone from the Justice Department or the FBI is willing to listen, and I think they will, then we'll point o the fishy business—pun intended—and give them my dad's records and let them do what they do."

Van shook his head. "These guys will sit on it forever. They'll drag it out with court orders, and wiretaps, and who knows what else. We don't have that type of time."

"I agree," Cat said. "We need to move faster."

Leo rubbed his chin. "What if we incentivize them to move faster?"

"How?" Van asked.

"Let me work that out for now. But I think if we can take down the Rocas in a public way, then the judge will have no choice but to take Chicho from them and deliver him into your hands."

"From your mouth," Cat said.

Anna wrote Permit on the wall. "We need to see if we can fast-track that piece, too. I'll check to see who we have in Sacramento who can pull strings for us. You've donated to enough of these people that one of them should be able to connect and accelerate."

"Perfect," Leo said.

"The nurse," Cat said. "Can we get access to her bank accounts? Break into her apartment or something? We need to see if she was murdered—"

"She was," Van interjected.

"Fine, why she was murdered? What did she know, and how does it tie to Lionel and us?"

"That will be much harder for us to track," Van said.

Leo studied Van. "But if we point the FBI in her direction as well..."

Van nodded. "Maybe."

Leo turned to Anna, who was already scribbling on the board.

"Finally," Anna said, "the ship and the boat that anchor just off this beach. What are they up to?"

"They are not selling illegally caught salmon, that's for sure," Cat said.

"Tomorrow morning," Anna said, "me and Van will walk that path they take on your property. Whatever is going on, they always take down the flimsy fence. Let's clean it up and hide cameras and whatnot. They are about due. I saw an episode about how these guys were trying to find Bigfoot, so they used some real cool tech. We should do the same."

Van nodded. "Bigfoot. Amazing."

"I'm not even sure what to say to that," Leo said.

"What? It's just mindless TV. I watch all that stuff."

"Kids, focus," Cat said. "Anything else?"

They all considered momentarily, then shook their heads.

"Back to what I started with, Cat," Leo said. "Let's not accelerate the next hearing. We need to allow some of these things to produce the information we need so that we can shake the hornet's nest."

"Whatever it takes," she said.

Leo studied her eyes. "I hope you mean that. Because what I have in mind will push all of us out of our comfort zones and into painfully uncomfortable zones."

Chapter Thirty-Nine

Anna

Anna and Van walked toward the gate on the pathway. They needed to establish a baseline. If the ship and boat were somehow associated with the situation at hand, then they would need to collect the information that would be needed for law enforcement.

Van had a rake, a sledgehammer, and a backpack filled with surveillance equipment. Anna also carried a backpack with some equipment.

He was about to smooth out the path when he paused and held Anna back. "Wait up," he said, then walked around the pathway in a large arc.

"What is it?"

He didn't speak for a few moments.

"Well?"

He glanced up at her. "Come here."

She did.

"Do you see these in the middle?"

She studied what were various indentations. "Are those footprints?"

"Yes. And the direction is from the beach toward...toward whatever is on the other side. Now look at these."

Approximately three feet on either side were more indentations, but they were larger and not as populated.

"Okay," she said, unsure what that meant.

"The ones on the outside look like men's boots." He leaned down to one nicely outlined print. The sand had been wet previously. The boot had left a clearly defined outline.

"Yeah, I can see that." She paused, studying the landscape some more. "So, men on the outside."

"Two, to be exact. One on either side."

She studied the indentations in the middle. Many of them. Much smaller. Her heartbeat accelerated.

"Look," he said, pointing to another area. Again, the wet sand had left better, clearer impressions.

"Bare feet?" Anna asked.

He pulled out a cigarette, put it between his lips, and lit it.

She tried to process what was happening. He had never smoked before. What did this mean?

"Yes. At best, women's feet." He took a long drag on his cigarette.

"At worst?"

He squeezed the lit tip of the cigarette, snuffing it out.

"At worst...children's feet."

They took pictures, smoothed out the sand, then installed various surveillance cameras. All was done in relative silence. The implications of what appeared to be in the sand weighed heavily on them.

"Let's see what this path takes us to," Van said. He stared at her. "Are you okay?"

"No," Anna said. "I think I'm gonna be sick."

Her voice got caught in her throat. A dam inside broke. She held her breath and squeezed the bridge of her nose.

He stepped up to her and brought her into an embrace.

That did it. She broke down, released some of the pain, then pulled away from him.

"I'm fine," she said.

"No. You're not. And you shouldn't be," he said. "This has taken a different turn. Listen to me carefully. We need to destroy them. With prejudice."

The way he spoke, the righteousness that he had in his tone, balanced with self-control, should've scared her. But he was one of the good guys. So, instead, what she felt rising inside her was strength.

"Amen," she said. "Let's see what we can find."

He extended his hand. She took it. He squeezed it and then walked up the sand dunes with her, hand in hand.

They'd defeat these people. Together.

Chapter Forty

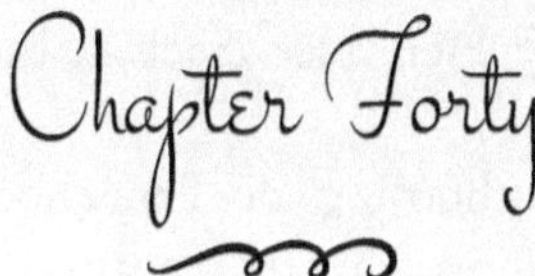

Catalina

Cat and Leo had pulled an all-nighter. She watched in awe as he built a database of the information she had produced and connected it to the database that his team had built from Lionel's journals. All she could do for much of the time was brew coffee and give him sustenance.

By midmorning, the data was producing the information that they had suspected would be discovered.

He leaned back in his chair. "My poor dad knew it was there, but he didn't have the tools or the technology to see what we're seeing now."

She stood behind a seated Leo. Her hands were on his shoulders, her face practically above his, studying the data.

"He knew you'd be able to bring it together," she said, then squeezed.

He swiveled the chair, causing her to trip into his lap. He pulled her in and stared up into her eyes.

"That was a fairly slick move, Mr. Moncrieff."

No wisecracks or witty comebacks. He just studied her eyes, melting her with each passing second.

She swallowed.

He pulled her in closer and tighter.

"Are you going to say something?" she asked, her voice low.

He shook his head. "Just want to take you in. Remember this moment. If I had only known earlier that choosing you would give me this much focus and joy."

"You've chosen me?" Her voice cracked, but she did not break eye contact.

"Every moment. I am choosing you. I am choosing me with you."

She smiled. "I don't know what that means."

He pulled her in and took her lips into his. Her hands went to his face, holding it, maneuvering it, accepting this moment of bliss as a gift. They tasted each other, allowed their instincts and their lost passion to arise once again.

But it wasn't like before. It was sweeter, with more urgency, a longing and a realization. A realization that a perfect melody can be lost if not protected.

He rose, lifting her in that same move, and walked her toward the back of her trailer.

She couldn't do this, but his lips were so perfect, the moment so beautifully arranged, that she wanted to throw all caution, all constraints out of the way and be with him again. Be with her first love.

He laid her on her bed and, in that moment, her eyes opened.

She put a hand on his lips.

He stopped.

She then pulled him next to her, and they faced each other.

"What's wrong?" he asked.

"Absolutely nothing," she said. "But it can't be like this. I can't do this."

His eyes showed his confusion.

"I am not the same person who I was when we were teenagers. I made a promise that I would no longer do things out of order."

"I'm so confused," he said.

"Lying next to you makes me want you more than ever. But we don't need to rush anything. Let's allow our kisses and our touches to be enough for now. God willing, my five-year-old will be back home soon. I am not going to just date. I am not going to just go there. Not even with you."

He blinked.

"Do you understand?"

He nodded. "So...you're saying we can still kiss?"

She smiled. He grinned back and brought her in for another round of constrained bliss. For now, this was all she could give him. She hoped he really understood. Because this felt right. It felt perfect.

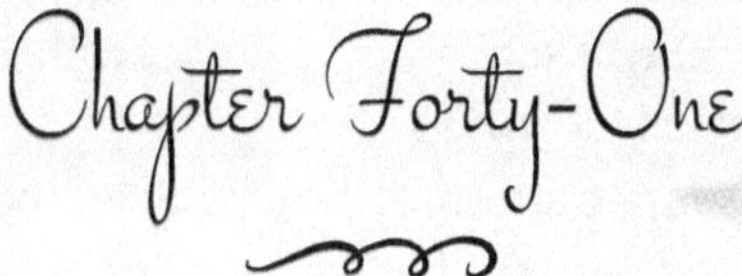

Chapter Forty-One

Leo

Leo and Cat listened with their mouths wide open. As Van explained what they had discovered and showed the pictures, Leo felt the taste of bile in his throat.

"So..." Cat started but shook her head first. "All these years, someone has been trafficking women and children right under our noses?"

Van nodded. "Most likely."

Anna wiped at her cheek. "It's disgusting. I don't even know where to begin and what to do. They are barefoot. These bastards want to make sure that these victims can't even attempt to run away."

Leo cleared his throat. "Where does the path go?"

"To the harbor. I would assume that on those days that the ship comes, the boat unloads them, they walk the two and a half miles to the harbor, and then...who knows. A bus? Another ship?"

"Who are the disgusting customers who are waiting for them?" Anna yelled. "I mean...this is freaking California. This type of stuff should not be happening."

Van sat. "Second most profitable illegal industry in the US. Second to narcotics."

Leo didn't know what to say and what to think. Only the wealthy could afford to do this. How many wealthy people did he personally know? Were some customers? He shook his head, not willing to believe that this was possible.

"I wonder," Cat said. "What was Rafa up to on that night? Was this the evolution he referred to?"

Leo rose, and grabbed a few beers, and passed them around. He took a long pull then connected his laptop.

"This helps explain a portion of how they are producing the income they need. I will just assume that the narcotics are what they've been doing for a long time and that they added human trafficking to increase their revenues. This would qualify under business development."

He pulled up the reports that they had generated earlier that day.

"They have built what appears like a perfectly architected money laundering operation."

Cat walked up to the screen and pointed to different data points.

"Here are the businesses they own, or have strong control over," Cat said. "Notice they are heavily cash-oriented businesses, minimal credit card slips. And they are ripe with opportunity to have high operating costs."

"And they also need continual renovations," Leo added. "So, their mainstay is the fishing businesses and harbor ownership. The fish are caught and sold almost always in cash.

"But they sell it to a distributor for way above market value. But they also own the distributor. So they are showing high costs and high revenues, inserting the illegal funds into the mix. Then they have to fix the harbor, the parks, the community, and the various businesses. But the contractor who is hired will charge ridiculous rates and they will get those bids. Why? Because the Rocas also own the contractors."

"Which explains why no one locally wanted to work on my home. They belong to the Rocas. They *are* the Rocas."

"We will not go beyond this," Leo closed his laptop. "This is enough for the master plan."

"Which is what, exactly?" Anna asked.

He grinned. "The master plan."

She was about to complain when he raised his hand.

"We have a plan. If this doesn't work, then there is no justice in this world."

As they all finished off their beers, Cat's phone rang.

Her eyes widened. "It's Pete Nicos," she said as she answered his video call and transmitted the feed to the TV screen.

"Wow, the entire team is here," Pete said.

"What news do you bring?" Leo asked.

"Does this have anything to do with what I sent you?" Cat's eyes were expectant.

Pete nodded, and a huge grin appeared. "It sure does!"

"What did you send him?" Anna asked.

"She sent me the solution to our problem."

"Go on. What is it?" Leo asked.

"Cat sent me old pictures from your ancestors during the construction of Casa. Cat, the moment I saw the pictures, I knew for sure that the woman in the middle with the shovel was Marion Hall. But what I needed to do was talk to a colleague who is an expert in her designs."

"Marion Hall is who exactly?" Leo asked.

"Considered among the top ten women architects in the US. She had worked with Frank Lloyd Wright and was mentored by Julia Morgan of Hearst Castle fame. She is a celebrated architect globally and is considered a jewel on the coast of California."

They all exchanged looks.

"So...what does that mean?" Cat asked.

"Every home that she has designed has been named a Historic home. The Neanderthals at the Fortuny Bay council who are requiring the demolishing of the building have lost all footing. It's not even their call anymore."

They all yelled and gave each other high fives.

"What's next?" Leo asked.

"Ball's already rolling. Some of the ideas we had may need to be modified to remain true to her design, but nothing out of the ordinary. Another cool tidbit. The ideas for extending the home—my colleague told me that those drawings have strokes from both Marion Hall and another person. Presumably your mother.

"Marion would've been very old by then, so one expert thought that those drawings may be one of her last sketches. So, for one, those sketches will be worth a few bucks. More importantly, from a generational perspective, your mom must've been something of a wunderkind that Marion would've collaborated with her. Congrats, team. We're going to rock this thing."

Leo just grinned. His amazing mother was more than just an amazing mother.

She was just plain and simply amazing.

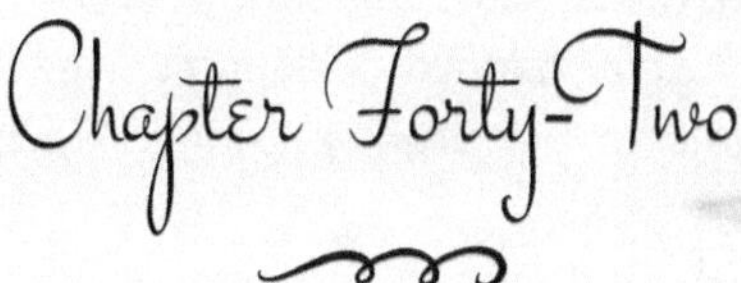

Chapter Forty-Two

Anna

Anna and Van walked up the stairs to Roberto Chaparral's office. After nearly five days, Leo gave them the okay to execute this phase of the conversation. The worm had done its job. Now they had to shake the nest.

The receptionist did not smile when they entered.

"I'm sorry, but Mr. Chaparral is very busy today," she said.

But as she said the rehearsed line, Chaparral stepped outside of his office and froze.

"Oh," is what he said.

"Mr. Chaparral," Anna said. "We're not here to stay or chat, but wanted to show you something that you'll definitely want to see."

His eyebrows furrowed. "What is it?"

She nodded toward his office.

He looked at his assistant, who shrugged then waved them in.

"Now, what is this about?" he asked.

Van handed him the papers that Roberto's assistant had printed. "You have a drum issue on your copier. You should change that."

Chaparral flinched. "This is what you wanted to tell me?"

The incredulity in his tone could be cut with a knife.

"Yes," Van said. "You see, a drum ghost line is nearly as good as a finger-print, when it comes to evidence."

"Evidence? What are you talking about?"

Van pulled out the newspaper articles that had been printed weeks ago and placed on Leo's windshield.

"Here you go." He handed Chaparral the printouts. "Notice anything?" He pointed to the drum ghosting. "Identical. I already had them analyzed."

Anna knew he had not done any such analysis. But she liked his style.

Roberto's gaze went from the printouts to Van's eyes, then Anna's.

"I don't know how...or who..."

"So you're saying your assistant may be the one doing the Rocas' bidding?" Anna asked. "I suppose anyone can be bought off. Not our issue to dig deep. We just present it to the right authority."

Roberto walked toward his desk as he continued to study the pages, one after another, after another.

"Not sure how this is a crime." He smiled, but his grin was faltering.

"Oh, this is not a crime," Anna said.

"Then we are on the same page."

She shook her head gently. "Not exactly. This isn't a crime. It just shows a deeply connected network to the Rocas. What is a crime is what we deci-phered from Lionel's hidden material."

Roberto dropped into his chair. "But...I don't understand." His voice was distant.

"Not very difficult," Anna said. "It's there in black and white. I'm sure you've studied the version that had been entrusted to you."

He blinked. Then shook his head, but there was no conviction behind it. "Articles. Just articles about businesses going under and people passing away... I don't understand."

His admission surprised her.

"There was nothing in there that was criminal," he said. "I wouldn't have kept his project away if there had been anything like that."

Anna sat in the chair in front of him. "Seems Lionel didn't give you the full version. What he gave you was a test of loyalty. Of friendship. You did not do so well."

He rose, running his hands through his hair.

Van narrowed the gap between him and her.

"I'm sorry," he said. "You need to leave now."

Anna rose, took the copies off his desk.

"Did you have to betray the family?" she asked.

His eyes turned red. "Betray another family or lose mine. Not a difficult choice."

Van and Anna huddled behind his computer monitor inside his car. Waiting. They had been waiting for Chaparral to leave, to do something. But so far, nothing.

After nearly two hours, an email account that was owned by Roberto Chaparral sent an email to an unknown address.

"They know. Be careful," is all it said.

They waited for more than an hour. The reply came.

"Meet me at the park."

Van turned on the engine and pulled the car a bit farther away. Within a couple of minutes, Chaparral's Mercedes-Benz pulled out of the parking structure. They followed him.

Roberto pulled into the same park that weeks earlier Anna and Van had used as their first meeting place. They waited.

A red Porsche pulled in and parked a few spaces away from Roberto's car.

The man stepped out.

"Son of a—" Van whispered, then clicked picture after picture.

The man was tall with thinning red hair. He walked with authority. Well-earned authority.

After all, he was a judge.

Chapter Forty-Three

Catalina

Cat sat in the back seat with Leo, both waiting on the call that had been just north of a week in the making.

"What's taking so long?" she asked.

He took her hand in his. He squeezed just hard enough to cause her to break her deadpan stare on the phone and turn to him.

"It's happening. Savor the moment."

At that, his phone rang. He tapped the speaker icon.

"The article is live," Anna said. "They are at the Roca estate."

He turned to her and winked. "Thanks, Anna."

He hung up.

"It's time," the man in the passenger seat said.

"You sure you don't want me to go in with you?" Leo asked Cat.

She grinned. "Positive. I got this."

"And Barb confirmed they're there?"

She nodded.

"Then do it."

"We'll have audio in here also," the man said.

He leaned in. "One for good luck."

She kissed him, stole some more of his confidence, then stepped out and marched toward the café's door.

As she opened it, she recalled the last time she'd been here for a meeting. The smells of tea, coffee, and pastry were the same. Unlike last time, this time the sounds of other guests added to the ambiance. Last time, they knew she was coming. This time, she was the one who would surprise them.

She pulled a chair and sat next to them. She crossed her legs.

Adela and Elizabeta turned to her. The look of disgust and shock was made for the cartoons.

"What the hell do you think you're doing here?" Elizabeta asked.

Cat smiled. "Came to give you a heads-up. But I recommend we clear out this place first."

"Leave us," Adela said to Cat. "I don't have time for you."

Cat crossed her arms. "You may want to hear it from me before you find out from another source."

Adela looked her up and down, studying her.

Elizabeta stood. "I'll drag you by your hair if you don't leave."

Cat nodded. "You could. And the press who's outside would love to get pictures of that."

"What press?" Elizabeta called one of her security guards, who looked out the window.

"What the—? I see a few people out there. Television from the look of it."

Elizabeta's jaw clenched so hard that for a second Cat thought her teeth would break.

"Clear the place," Adela said, and immediately patrons were ushered out of here.

Cat's breathing was getting a bit labored. With each second, her heartbeat hammered harder. Her throat constricted, and her tongue felt like it was getting thicker.

You can do this, she reminded herself. *This is their last dance.*

Barb told the patrons that they would not have to pay for their unfinished breakfasts.

Once all were gone, Cat told Barb, "It's best for you and the staff to leave also."

Within a minute, all were gone, and all who remained were Cat, Adela, and Elizabeta.

"Thank you for the theatrics," Adela said. "Now, speak!"

"As we sit, an article hit the *Wall Street Journal* and the *New York Times*. At the same time, a coordinated launch of thousands of posts is hitting all social medial platforms."

"An article?" Adela asked.

"Yes. The title is 'A Family of Corruption and Trafficking.' I would've picked something more direct, like 'Adela Roca and her daughter are evil.' But I did not have a say."

"What is this?" Elizabeta said. "You've written an article about our family. And you think it'll hold?"

"I haven't written anything. The journalist is a Pulitzer Prize winner, apparently. I saw the pre-publication draft. He's fairly good."

Elizabeta pulled out her phone. Messages were coming in.

"Furthermore, the FBI is currently doing what they do best. Entering all your businesses and taking documents. I think they have also coordinated visits to your Mexico operation. More importantly, they are also at your home."

Adela was aging in front of her own eyes. "How dare you? You are a bug. A nothing. A—"

The door opened, and state police, along with agents entered. They quickly took Adela's security away, then stood by Cat.

"Ma'am, we need to process them," the agent said.

"Thank you for letting me do this. I just have one more thing I want to say." She took a deep breath. "I am about to get my son back. I suspect Judge McAuliffe is about to call an unplanned session. But over the last week, I've been thinking about your son."

Her eyes turned to Elizabeta.

"Don't you dare defile him by using his name in that filthy mouth of yours."

Cat didn't bite. "I've been thinking about what it was that he had to take care of that night. I asked him to not go. I had a bad feeling about it. I even asked you, Adela, to stop him. To talk some sense into him. After all, he respected you."

Adela stared at Cat.

"And you told me you'd take care of it. I think you did. I have no evidence, but I suspect he found out about the sex trafficking and child trafficking. And even though I bet he didn't hesitate in bringing narcotics here, I think even he had a line. Maybe he took after his father. So I suspect..."

"What?" Elizabeta asked, but her voice was lower now.

"I suspect your mother got rid of your son, because he was about to spoil the party." Cat rose. "I don't know if this is true, but I wouldn't put it past your family to kill one of your own. You've done it before. You chew on that and see if the pieces fit. Maybe they do. Maybe they don't.

"As for me, this is the version that I will tell my son, my Chicho. I want him to know that his father was a deeply flawed man, but as his last act, he decided to do good. He wasn't a good man. But maybe in that last moment, when he realized he had been poisoned, he found an opportunity to ask God for forgiveness."

Old memories flashed through her mind. "He used to make fun of me for believing and praying. But I think most people, when they hit bottom, and they realize they only have one last note in their melody, they turn to a source higher than themselves."

Elizabeta faced her mother. Adela did not blink.

Cat smiled, then walked out.

Today was a good day.

Chapter Forty-Four

Leo

Leo rushed out of the agent's car and waited for Cat to emerge out of the café. As she walked out, when she made eye contact with him, she smiled and walked into his embrace.

He held her tightly and rocked her gently. Against his chest, he felt her release as she and cried softly.

She pulled back and wiped her cheeks. He had not seen that perfect smile for way too long.

"You did it," he said.

She shook her head. "I couldn't have done it without my team."

He placed his arm around her shoulder and walked toward the lead FBI investigator. They shook hands, then parted company.

"Thank you for letting us do this," Leo said. "I owe you one."

The agent grinned. "And I'll be sure to collect."

Leo winked and walked away. As much as he hated to sell his soul to the feds, this had to be done.

They waited in the Cybertruck and watched as Adela and Elizabeta walked out in cuffs and were ushered into cars.

"Never thought I'd see the day," she said.

Her phone rang. She pulled it out and then showed it to Leo.

"Let's see what your attorney wants to say," he said.

"What just happened?" Zareh asked.

"Why would you ask that?" Cat asked.

"For one, the reports all over about the Roca family and also the call that I got from the court. They want me there for an emergency session. Looks like Judge McAuliffe has told CPS to return Francisco to his mother."

Leo leaned back and laughed. "I bet he has."

Cat's hands flew to her face and she broke down. She cried and laughed and gasped for air. He pulled her into his chest and in that moment, he believed he was experiencing her joy through her.

After she hung up, she grabbed his hand. "Within the hour, I'll get my baby back."

"Within the hour, your life and Chicho's life will be back under your control. Without the Roca cloud hovering over your shoulder. You can do whatever you want at this point. You don't even have to stay here if you don't want."

She studied him. "No way. We stay. We turn Fortuny Bay into what your family line envisioned over a hundred years ago. Not what the Rocas created."

"Good decision. Very good decision."

Epilogue

Catalina

Cat raised her hand to block the sun's glare. She studied the framework that was going up on the wings of Casa Moncrieff. It was going to look beautiful.

"When do we live inside the big house again, Mom?"

"Maybe in six months, Chicho."

"Six months!" he said with such drama that she thought she might have accidentally said six years.

"It'll go by very fast. You'll see."

He didn't look convinced.

But time was flying. In the weeks following the arrest of Adela and the family, more pieces had fallen into place. Roberto had turned and given the feds evidence. What would happen to him? She did not know. The fire inspector had also reappeared and provided phone recordings of the threats he had received. Deputy Billy was no longer a deputy. Details had not been shared.

And Nurse Maria had done wrong by Lionel. She had been paid handsomely to only give one unit of blood at each appointment. They had purposely given him less than Lionel needed to survive and thrive.

Cat no longer thought of these people. God would deal with them. Leo wanted to personally deal with them. But he had agreed on the compromise —let the law punish and shame them.

"Ready to go to the beach?" she asked.

"I wanna wait for Leo."

"He knows where we're going. He'll find us."

He shrugged. "I wanna wait."

"Fine. We wait."

Just then, Leo strutted toward them. He wore board shorts, ridiculously expensive sandals, and no top. If he was trying to make her look at his body, it wasn't going to work.

Oh, who was she kidding? Of course it worked. But she would not give him the satisfaction.

He draped the towel around his shoulder and waved. "All ready?"

"Been waiting for you forever," Cat said.

"Not forever, Mom. That's just silly."

"Silly mom," Leo said, and gave her a wink. "Before we go, I was thinking right over there would be perfect."

He pointed to a location some fifty yards away from the house overlooking the ocean.

"For what? Your statue?" she asked.

"Ha. Haha. Funny. No, I was thinking of an event lawn rotunda. Walk with me."

They all followed him.

"What event are we planning on having here? It's fairly low priority, I'd say."

"Well, the most important type of events, of course. Weddings. This will be the place to go to for exclusive, not too big, not too small, celebrity-type people's weddings. A perfect beach, outdoor ceremony, and dining. In a few months, all the trees will build up nice privacy. It will be ideal."

She looked around and could see his point. "I suppose. But maybe for phase two or three? We can talk to Pete about it."

He shook his head, unconvinced.

"What?" she asked.

He slipped something off his pinky, and he held it in front of her.

"The thing is, I think we'll need it sooner."

She stared at the ring. His old promise ring. "Did you snake that off my keychain?"

"Well, yes. It was mine. Which I gave to you, tied to a promise that I did not keep. So...it's time."

She stared at him. "Time for what?"

From his pocket, he produced another ring. His mother's ring.

She looked into his eyes. Then back to the ring.

"What are you doing?" she asked.

"Marry me. Let's do this thing the right way. The three of us as one family."

She blinked, barely able to breathe, much less speak.

Something tugged at her sundress. She looked down.

Chicho smiled up at her. "I knew what he was going to do. And I promised not to tell you anything."

Leo lifted him off the ground and nestled him on his hip.

"You haven't actually given us an answer yet."

"Yes. Absolutely yes." She grabbed his face and kissed him. Just as she was about to get lost in the moment, a pair of wet lips kissed her cheek.

She turned and faced Chicho. "What are you doing?"

"Kissing you."

He grinned.

The three of them melded into an embrace. There was a lot that still had to be sorted. Lawyers and courtrooms would be in their foreseeable future. Also, the town needed to heal and recover from a decade of manipulation and torment.

But she had Chicho and Leo. And with this house perching over Fortuny Bay, this town would have a legitimate shot at being a great place again.

A place of fortunes.

— The End —

That's the end of the Fortuny Bay series (for now...). Thank you for reading this duet. If you want to read a redemption story of a tennis celebrity, then you'll want to click over to **Game of Love***, Book 1 in the Second Chance Coast series.*

Please Leave a Review!

If you enjoyed this book, you can make a big difference by leaving a review.

Honest reviews of my books help in getting the attention of new readers.

To leave a review, return to the retailer's website, search for SECRETS AT FORTUNY BAY, and leave an honest review.

Thank you!

Join Ara's V.I.P. Club

Ara Grigorian's VIP Club members receive free behind the scenes content to accompany the book.

Members are always the first to hear about Ara's new books and publications.

Click to Join my VIP Club:
www.AraGrigorian.com

Books by Ara Grigorian

Second Chance Coast Series

Game of Love

Ten Year Dance

15 Days With You

***

Fortuny Bay Series

Reunion at Fortuny Bay

Secrets of Fortuny Bay

Author's Notes

There's a saying about best laid plans. I can't recall what the actual saying says, but if it implies your plans are meaningless, then I have experienced it first hand.

Give that, the first thing I have to do is apologize to my readers.

I had originally intended this series to be a trilogy. Book 2 would come in late summer of 2022 and book 3 in late winter of 2022. That did not happen. The trilogy became a duet and the release date slipped into early Spring of 2023.

There are many excuses — some legitimate (a lot of family health matters), some less so (not enough coffee and Nutella at home). But in the end, the delay was because I was not happy with the story.

I had finished book 2 in the summer of '22. But despite praises from my first readers, something didn't feel right. While I waited for the edits to come back for book 2, I began working on book 3. That's when it hit me. I'm forcing this to become three books. This is a duet, not a trilogy. Cat and Leo's story needed to come to a conclusion in book 2.

So I tossed half the book away and I got to writing the real book 2 in early 2023. By the time I was done, I knew I had made the right call.

As happy as I am with the book, it all happened at the worst time. My dear cat of nearly 14 years passed away in late February. Leo was my ever present companion who I miss dearly.

Yes, you guessed it, some of my characters are named or inspired by my amazing cats. Pete and Sophie from Ten Year Dance for example. And Leo, the Cat, for this series.

It hurts, I won't lie. He has been with me, sitting outside my office through all my books. I know he's in heaven in my home there. And that gives me peace.

So thank you for your understanding. And for your support. I hope you like this book. I hope you had fun with this duet.

Having said that, I have not eliminated the possibility that there will be more books in the Fortuny Bay series. It's just that for now, Cat and Leo have their story problem resolved. But that town has a lot more stories to reveal.

Thank you, as always, for being my readers. I could not do this without you.

Acknowledgments

Special thanks to my alpha and beta readers: Andreh Anderson, Norm Thoeming, and Janis Thomas. You guys rock!

My first reader: my wife. As our son's often ask, "How did you land mom?" :) I don't know. But I am forever grateful that we found each other.

My cover designer, Tracy Van Dolder of Virtually Possible Designs. Thank you for your insight and creativity. You see through my thoughts and deliver the best.

Armen Melik-Abramians of FlashCube Photography for the awesome headshot.

Armen Melik-Abramians for asking the uncomfortable questions that you asked the doctors on my behalf that helped me assure what I wrote was medically accurate.

Michael Steven Gregory of the Southern California Writers' Conference (Irvine and San Diego): Thank you for what you do to make it possible for writers to write more and suck less! And thank you for your friendship.

My friends and family: I love you.

To my fans: I love you, too!

Fight the good fight!

About the Author

Author's photo courtesy of FlashCube Photography © 2021

Ara Grigorian is a USA Today Bestselling author whose novels include the international award-winning Game of Love, Ten Year Dance, 15 Days With You, Desire After Dark (anthology), Reunion at Fortuny Bay and Secrets at Fortuny Bay, his latest series. Fascinated by the human species, Ara writes about choices, relationships, and second chances. Always a sucker for a hopeful ending, he writes contemporary stories targeted to adult and new adult readers.

Ara is also a technology executive in the entertainment industry. He earned his Master's in Business Administration from University of Southern California. True to the Hollywood life, Ara wrote for a children's television pilot that could have made him rich (but didn't) and nearly sold a video game to a major publisher (who closed shop days later). Ara and his wife are the proud parents of two teenage boys and two senior cats. They have laid roots in both Los Angeles and North Dallas.

Ara is a story coach and a workshop leader. He has taught at the Southern California Writers' Conference, Santa Barbara Writers Conference, the Writer's Digest Novel Writing Conference, and many others.

Ara is represented by Stacey Donaghy of Donaghy Literary Agency.

www.AraGrigorian.com